Shuffling t  y
finally ca
green vase.

He held it up, fairly certain it hadn't seen use in years. "Don't get a lot of flowers, do you, Blair?"

"Nope." Her voice softened, fading to a murmur as she set the table. "Mine usually come from the yard, and it's generally Sam bringing them to me."

He shoved the flowers into the water and tried not to think of anything but the reason he was standing at her sink.

Watching her under the curtain of his lashes, he felt a familiar stab of emotion. Folding napkins and placing them on the table, Blair obviously had no idea of the picture of domestic happiness she presented to him.

He blinked, focusing his attention on the dark green vase in front of him.

Set the flowers on the counter.

Look out the window.

Do any of a hundred meaningless things to take your mind off her. Just don't let her get to you. Don't fall in love again.

No, he definitely would not fall in love with her again. He couldn't. He'd come tonight only to find out why.

KATHLEEN Y'BARBO is an award-winning novelist and sixth-generation Texan. After completing a degree in marketing at Texas A&M University, she spent the next decade and a half raising children (four) and living with her engineer husband in such diverse places as Lafayette, Louisiana; Port Neches, Texas; and Jakarta, Indonesia. She now lives with her nearly grown brood near Houston, Texas, where she is active in Fellowship of the Woodlands Church as well as being a member of American Christian Romance Writers, Romance Writers of America, and the Houston Writer's Guild. She also writes a monthly column in the local RWA chapter newsletter and lectures on the craft of writing at the elementary and secondary levels.

Books by Kathleen Y'Barbo

HEARTSONG PRESENTS
HP474—You Can't Buy Love

Major League Dad

Kathleen Y'Barbo

Heartsong Presents

To Jacob, the real Sam
"Above all, love each other deeply,
because love covers over a multitude of sins."
1 Peter 4:8 NIV

A note from the author:
*I love to hear from my readers! You may correspond with me
by writing:*

Kathleen Y'Barbo
Author Relations
PO Box 719
Uhrichsville, OH 44683

ISBN 1-58660-743-X

MAJOR LEAGUE DAD

one

Mason Walker stood on the corner of Prairie and Vine and watched the traffic coming from both directions. In exactly ten minutes Blair Montgomery would walk back into his life just as they'd planned seven months ago on the day of their divorce.

He stared at the hands of the clock atop the bank building and willed them to move faster. Ten minutes became nine, then eight. Finally, with seven minutes left until noon, Mason paused to allow an ambulance to scream past, then crossed Prairie to take his place on the green and red bench outside Luigi's Italian Café.

Placing a dozen yellow roses on the seat beside him, Mason glanced at his reflection in the plate glass window that faced downtown. It had taken some fast talking to get his twenty-four-hour pass from the team, and he'd have to miss playing in tonight's game against the Astros, but none of those things mattered. He had a ring in his coat pocket and a goal in his mind.

Tonight he and Blair would take the next step toward becoming husband and wife again, and this time no man or woman, not even Lettie James, would keep them apart.

The rest of his life—the best of his life—would begin in five minutes.

❧

"ETA five minutes," the emergency medical technician shouted

5

over the roar of the siren. "I have a white, pregnant female, unconscious, victim of auto pedestrian accident. BP is low, pulse rate high. Showing signs of advanced labor."

"Roger that, Unit 14. Any ID?"

"Montgomery," he said as the ambulance turned sharply and lurched forward. "Blair Montgomery."

≈

"Blair Montgomery, please." Mason steeled himself for the tirade he knew Blair's grandmother was about to unleash. Still, with Blair nearly a half hour late, he had to try to find her.

Surely there was an explanation for her tardiness. In their brief phone conversation last week, the only contact he'd had with her since their parting, she'd sounded happy to be seeing him again. She wanted him to see something, something so special, she'd claimed, that she couldn't say what it was over the phone.

"That you, Mason Walker?"

Mason took a deep breath and let it out slowly. "Yes, Ma'am, it is. I was just wondering if your granddaughter might be there."

Silence.

"Mrs. James?"

"Yeah, I'm here." She paused. "Look a-here, Boy. Blair ain't got no interest in you no more. Just you leave her be, you hear?"

"I can't do that."

"Well, you'd better, or her new husband might not appreciate it."

≈

Lettie James hung up the phone and reached for her car keys. The good Lord hadn't given her Blair only to let her lose her to the likes of a Yankee fool, especially not one who'd never spent a day at hard work or a Sunday inside a church.

Her grandbaby and great-grandbaby deserved better'n that.

The nice doctor down at the Hermann Hospital had said Blair would be out of surgery and in recovery soon, so she'd better scoot.

Later on, when Blair was better, she'd break the news to her about that good-for-nothing Mason Walker and how he had called to cancel their little shindig at the Italian place over on Prairie. She'd smart a bit at first, but Grandma Lettie would be there to help pick up the pieces.

"It's all for the best, Blair, Honey." She closed the door behind her and headed for the Buick. And if her part in this ever came out, she'd just have to tell 'em both she'd done it for love.

After all, the Good Book says that everyone ought to love each other, on account of love covering a multitude of sins.

one

Something told Mason Walker to stop, turn around, and look. When he did, he saw her.

At least he thought it was Blair Montgomery. Maybe the combination of Tennessee heat and painkillers he'd taken for his bad knee had hit him too hard. He blinked, shaking his head before training his gaze on her again.

His heart slammed against his chest. It was her. Blair.

She appeared out of nowhere, an image out of his past, painful and still fresh after all these years.

The game.

Mason almost forgot he should be watching the game. A volunteer third-base coach had no business forgetting his responsibilities, even if the only woman he'd ever loved sat fewer than twenty yards away, acting as if she didn't recognize him. Their gazes met, and Blair quickly looked away.

He cast another furtive glance in her direction. From where he stood, she looked every bit as beautiful as the last time he'd seen her. That day haunted him still.

If only he'd torn up the divorce papers and made her stay instead of allowing her to flee their marriage. If only he'd known the Lord then, maybe—

"Mason! Hey, Buddy!" Trey demanded. "Get your head in the game!"

He looked up in time to see a pint-sized ballplayer running toward him at full speed. Motioning for him to run for home, he watched as the boy slid past the catcher and rose triumphantly.

"And that's the tie-breaker!" the announcer shouted.

The folks began to cheer as the run ended the game. Mason looked over at the place where Blair had been sitting. She was gone.

"Get a grip, Buddy. You lock like you've seen a ghost," he heard Trey say. He tried to shake off the image, but all Mason could get rid of was Trey's hold on his shoulder as they walked off the field together.

Without looking back, he climbed into the rented Jeep, gunned the engine, and headed for the interstate. Maybe if he drove fast enough and prayed hard enough, he could leave her memory behind in the tree-shaded ballpark.

Unfortunately, it didn't work. When he opened the door to his Knoxville hotel suite fifteen minutes later, the feeling chased him inside. Now that he'd seen her again, what would he do about it? And what would she say if he tried to contact her? How would she react to his intrusion into her apparently well-ordered suburban life? That was the most disturbing question of all, and for it he had no answer.

After all, it had been nearly ten years.

He hated to think of those days, and most times he squashed the thoughts before they took over. But tonight as he sat in the presidential suite of the most expensive hotel around, he found his usual self-control had eluded him.

His mind, so long closed to that part of his life, now roamed freely down dangerous corridors of the past, and memories rose unbidden to the surface. A door he had shut many years ago now stood wide open. It hurt something awful, but Mason stepped through and let the images swirl around him.

Five minutes after he had arrived in town, Mason had wondered why transferring to this college in the heart of central Texas had ever seemed like a good idea.

Then he found Blair Montgomery and fell in love.

For the better part of four glorious weeks, they had been Mr. and Mrs. Mason Walker, and the sum total of their possessions could have fit easily in the back of his pickup.

Then came the reality that being married was hard and getting a divorce to solve their problems was easy.

How was I ever so naïve, Lord? Why did I think everything was so simple? If only I'd known You then.

The phone rang and chased away the fog of memories. Mason walked toward it slowly, hoping whoever it was would give up and go away. Finally, when he reached the desk in the opposite corner of the room, he allowed the phone to ring once more before picking it up.

"Walker, what's this I hear about a baseball camp?"

"Well, good evening, Morty. How's everything out on the coast?" He smiled, knowing his lack of reaction would only increase his agent's anger.

"Good evening, yourself. If you're looking to blow the negotiations on your contract extension with the Honolulu Waves, just keep on doing what you're doing."

Mason allowed a long moment of silence to come between them before answering. "Morty, I have no idea what you're talking about."

"Nice try. I know you're down there working some kiddy camp when you should be up in Montana at that pitiful cabin of yours signing baseballs and letting your knee heal."

"Aw, it's no big deal. I've got a flight out tomorrow." Mason hauled the cordless phone back out onto the patio. "Besides, all I do is stand around and look useful—I promise."

"Don't promise me anything you don't. . ."

Mason set the phone down on the wrought-iron and glass table, pulled his T-shirt over his head, and let it fall. When he settled into the lounge chair and picked up the phone once more, his agent was still talking.

". . .and with another contract in the works you can't be taking these stupid chances. I'm only looking out for your interests here. You know that, don't you, Mason?"

He closed his eyes, savoring the feel of the sun as it peeked out from behind a particularly ominous-looking cloud. The wind smelled of rain, which made him think of Blair all over again. He frowned and shook his head, as if the thoughts could be easily dislodged.

"Walker, answer me."

A small beep punctuated his agent's outburst. Could Blair have recognized him at the park and traced him through Trey to this hotel?

"Sorry, Morty," he said. "Gotta go. Someone's trying to get through."

"That someone is me, Buddy, and if my message doesn't get through, you're going to be blowing a sweet ten-million-dollar deal."

Another beep.

"Don't even joke about that," Mason said, adding an edge to his voice that he hoped his agent wouldn't miss. "You just get me the money, all right? I'll take care of the rest."

A third beep. Blair could be about to give up.

"I still think—"

"Bye, Morty!" He pushed the button before the enraged man could continue. "Mason Walker here."

"Hey, Pal, how would you like me to make your day?" Trey paused, obviously waiting for a reaction.

Mason suppressed the desire to do his best Clint Eastwood impression, opting for a simple grunt of agreement instead.

"I found Blair."

A knot formed in his throat, making words impossible.

"Mase? You there?"

Silence.

"Hey, Mase! Did you hear what I said? Talk to me, Pal."

"Yeah," he managed. "Uh, sorry. I, uh, I—" He closed his eyes and said a prayer for guidance before he practiced the words in his head. Finally, he attempted the nearly impossible task of saying them aloud. "Where is she?"

"Lives out in Magnolia," he said. "Has a landscape architecture business."

So Blair had gone into the landscape business as she'd planned. Well, good for her. Strange she'd gone all the way from Texas to Tennessee to do it. Maybe her husband had a job transfer.

The husband. He hated to ask, but he had to.

"Is she still married?" He ground out the words, afraid of the answer. The wait for a response nearly killed him.

"Nothing about a husband on the forms. Looks like she's a free agent, Buddy."

Finally, Mason managed a ragged breath. "Give me her number." He opened the desk drawer and fished around for a pen. "On second thought just give me her address. This is one reunion that ought to take place face-to-face."

Half an hour later, Mason headed up the freeway with his favorite CD in the stereo and the windows rolled down. As he banged his hand against the steering wheel in time to the music, Mason refused to consider what he might find at his destination. Instead he turned the matter over to the Lord and concentrated on the music and, more rarely, the map.

"Uh-oh," he muttered under his breath when he almost missed the blacktop leading north.

A pair of deer skittered across the road in front of him, causing Mason to slam his foot on the brakes. He pulled the Jeep to the side of the deserted highway, threw it into park, and leaned back against the seat. The sounds of the night came at him from all angles, even over the soft purring of the engine.

The deer disappeared from the glow of the headlights, leaving nothing but a dark, empty circle of highway in front of him. He stared hard at that circle and tried to make sense of his scattered thoughts.

Up the road lived the most important woman in his life, the only one who'd managed to love him despite all his faults. The only one who hadn't cared about his batting average or how much money he made.

The only one who'd ever hurt him.

Mason squared his shoulders and kicked the car into drive. Too soon he saw the sign that indicated he'd reached her street.

He eased the car down the road, immediately relieved there were no streetlights to illuminate him. Suppressing the wild desire to cut the headlights and coast the remaining distance to her, Mason touched the accelerator lightly, his gaze fastened on the blue and white mailbox bearing the reflective numbers for which he'd been searching.

Whatever possessed him at that moment, he would never know. Without turning his head in the direction of the house, he sped past it, gunning the engine and leaving a spray of black pebbles in his wake.

Safely away from her, he slowed down and removed his foot from the gas, allowing the Jeep to coast to a stop. Before he could think, he threw the vehicle in reverse and turned around, facing back in the direction of her house. He cut the headlights and shut off the engine.

It was crazy, and he knew it, this urge to find her again, especially since she'd obviously spent no energy worrying about where he might be. Mason gave in to the feeling anyway, wanting to see her but not exactly sure what he would say when he did.

Better to do this without her knowing, he decided, as he climbed out of the Jeep and headed toward her house on foot. The sound of his boot heels hitting the road punctuated the soft hum of the crickets.

His strides lengthened when the mailbox came into view again. A moment later, he broke into a run, not realizing it until he had arrived at his destination. Too late he felt his knee start throbbing as the air in his lungs burned like fire.

He leaned against the white picket fence and fought for each gasp of breath forced into his lungs. A movement caught his attention, taking his mind off the excruciating pain shooting through his leg.

Framed by the warm, golden glow of lamplight, he could make out only the dimmest of silhouettes. But he knew it was Blair. He felt her, even before he could see clearly.

As if she'd sensed his presence, she walked toward him. A moment later, her face became visible in the square white picture frame of the window.

White curtains moved against the soft evening breeze, rustling about her as she stood there clutching what looked like a book to her chest. From somewhere inside, soft music floated across the small lawn toward him. Mason took another breath, all physical pain forgotten as he contemplated the image.

A light went on in the room upstairs, drawing his attention away from her. The movement of two shadows played against the creamy window shade until the shade flew open, carving a bright square of light into the front yard only inches from Mason's boots. Instinctively, he stepped back.

A small, fair-haired boy in red-and-white striped pajamas leaned his elbows against the windowsill, his chin tilting skyward. "Up there's Orion." The boy pointed up at the stars, his childish voice carrying across the yard to where Mason stood. The dog beside him looked toward the heavens as if he understood. "And there's the Little Dipper."

Then Blair appeared next to the boy, and Mason was lost once more. Nothing in all the memories he had of Blair prepared him for the sight of her with the tow-headed boy in her arms.

Yet all he could think of was that the boy should have been his. And she should have still been his wife.

Then he realized what had stopped him from stepping back into her life again. She wasn't his wife anymore. That distinction had gone to another.

What was he doing there? Why had he driven all this way to stand in Blair's front yard and act like a lovesick fool?

He was losing it, for sure. And on top of that, his bum knee felt as if it had been mangled under the wheels of a Mack truck. Time to go back to the hotel and speak to the Lord a bit. He'd try to pretend this night had never happened.

"G'night, Mom." The childish voice drifted on the breeze, sinking into his brain and wrapping itself around Mason's battle-scarred heart. "I love you."

" 'Night, Sweetie," he heard Blair say. "I love you too."

The words beckoned to him, pulled him out of the shadows and onto the cracked sidewalk that led to her door. He'd almost reached the doorbell when he realized what he had done and froze.

He closed his eyes and took his fears to the Lord. *Blair and I need to have a real conversation sometime, don't we, Lord? It might as well be now, right?*

When no answer came, Mason extended his index finger until he'd almost touched the doorbell.

"G'night, Daddy." The words floated across the porch like a soft breeze. "Do you know I love you?"

Mason didn't wait around to hear the answer.

two

Blair prepared Sam for bed while her mind raced and her heart threatened to splinter each time her son said his name.

Mason. So much time had passed, and so much pain still remained. Things were going so well. *Why did You let him see me today at the ballpark, Lord?*

She tossed a damp towel across the hamper and surveyed the tiny bathroom. As usual, Sam had done his best to brush his teeth and wash his face after his bath, but his cleanup had left a little to be desired. Wet footsteps led from the tub to the sink where they stopped at the blue floral rug. A blob of green toothpaste decorated the sink, and the door to the medicine cabinet stood open.

Blair closed the medicine cabinet and caught a glimpse of her haggard expression in the mirror. She snapped off the light.

"Mason Walker called me a slugger today at camp, Mom. He's awesome."

Sam's words echoed in her ears long after the nine-year-old boy had stepped out of the tub and dashed to his room in fresh pajamas with his newly autographed, red baseball cap still on his head. Taking one last look, Blair peeked into the darkened room and saw that, even in his sleep, he still wore the cap. A suspicious lump moved beneath the covers, and Sam lifted a hand to still it. His eyes never opened, although Blair now realized he could not be asleep.

She flipped on the light and tried to look stern. "Get the dog out of the bed, Sam. You know the rules."

Slowly, he peeled the covers back to reveal the mutt he'd

hidden there. "Sorry, Bubba," he said. "You gotta go sleep in the kitchen."

The furball slid off the bed and slunk past Blair. She knew he would return as soon as she left the room, but at the moment a misbehaving dog was the least of her worries.

"Wanna say prayers with me, Mom?"

"First, let's talk about something." She stepped over his cleats and bag to straighten the denim quilt and fluff his pillow. Dropping to one knee, she took a deep breath and let it out slowly, hoping the right words would come. "It's about the baseball camp."

"It's so cool." He bolted upright, eyes wide. "I can't believe Mason Walker's really there. I always watch him on television, and once I—"

"Sam, I don't think you can go back to camp tomorrow."

Before she'd finished the statement, tears had begun to gather, both hers and his. She felt another break in the armor surrounding her heart.

His *why* came like a soft, sweet whisper.

Why indeed? She certainly couldn't tell him the real reason. "Because I don't think it's a good idea."

A tear slid down his cheek, skirting a path across his freckles to drop onto the denim quilt he clutched beneath his chin. "But why?"

Several perfectly valid reasons came to her mind, first and foremost the distinct possibility her son could once again come into direct contact with his father. Blair forced a smile and blinked back the shimmering of tears threatening to fall.

"Well, I've got so much work to do and—"

"I can help you with your work after camp. You like it when I go on your jobs, and I can water the plants just like you taught me, and I'll even—"

"Sam," she said slowly. "Enough."

His bottom lip trembled, and he sniffed loudly. "But I don't see why I can't go. All we did today was a hitting clinic, then we played a game."

"Well, that sounds like a lot of fun," she offered.

"Yeah, but tomorrow, since Mr. Walker won't be there, we're going to practice pitching and catching, and you know how I wanna learn to catch."

He swiped at his cheek with the quilt, then focused his blue gaze on her. For a split second, she saw his father in his eyes. Looking away, she fumbled with the blankets until the impact of his statement hit her.

"You mean Mr. Walker's not going to be there tomorrow?" She worked at making the words sound as innocent as possible. "I thought he was part of the camp staff."

He straightened his cap and peered at her from under the brim. "Naw, he just came for today on account of his knee is hurt, and he has to go back to his team or something." Making a face, he shook his head. "The Wild Man's not a catcher, Mom."

No, but his friend Trey is.

Intending to tell the boy he would be anywhere but at baseball camp tomorrow, she looked straight at him and somehow said, "You're right. There's no good reason why you can't go."

The smile dawning on his face sealed the cracked edges of her resolve. Of course. Trey might be Mason's friend, but he would be far too busy to care that she had a son at camp. Not allowing Sam to return might cause more consternation, where pretending all was well might keep them above suspicion.

Besides, she reasoned as she pretended not to notice Sam's mutt slinking back into the room, surely she hadn't come this far to be found out now.

"Now can we say prayers, Mom?"

Blair smoothed the quilt around her son. "You go ahead," she whispered through the constriction in her throat. "Tonight I'll just listen and agree."

"Dear Lord, thank You for talking Mom into letting me go

to camp tomorrow, and I hope You'll make it as good a day as it was today. Please bless Mom and. . ."

&a

June 21

Last night, when Sam prayed, Blair had felt an unexplainable hope take wing. It stayed with her through the bedtime routine and followed her into the kitchen for cereal and milk at dawn. All through the morning, as she dealt with the details of work, she nurtured that hope.

When tax forms and blueprints for new client Griffin Davenport's atrium could no longer hold her interest, she gave into her worries and took them outside to her potting shed. There she began to give her Varigated Liriope a long overdue change of containers. Still, even as she sat up to her elbows in peat moss and potting soil, her mind traveled to the ballpark and Sam, and her prayers went with him. Surely God wouldn't let her decision to send Sam there today be a wrong one.

Not after she'd spent half the night crying and the other half in prayer.

That thought alone kept her going. Davenport, a real estate mogul, had proved to be quite an exacting client. "Demanding but fair," she whispered as she reached for her container of pearlite and mixed the tiny white pellets with soil. Garnering his approval was something she did not take lightly. A man in his position could make or break her fledgling career.

Pondering the points of that statement took less than a moment. "Only God can make or break my career," she reminded herself. She wiped the perspiration from her brow and returned to work on the task at hand.

Then, a few minutes before noon, the phone rang, and Mason Walker's voice greeted her with a polite hello. Her good feelings faded, as did her ideas for Griffin Davenport's blueprints. A cold emptiness and an even colder voice, her own, replaced them.

"Mason?" The clay pot in her hand hit the floor. "Sam told me you'd left."

"Yeah, I was supposed to." He paused briefly. "Um, Sam Montgomery—he's yours, right?"

Blair picked her way around the shattered pieces of terra cotta and with a trembling hand reached for the broom. "Yes." The words *and yours* came to mind, and she nearly dropped the phone too.

"Well, he's a tough guy," Mason said slowly, "but he kind of needs his mom right now."

❧

Mason hung the phone up and eased down beside the injured boy. Still reeling from the sound of the familiar voice, he offered Sam a tentative smile.

He and Blair were bound to run into each other before camp was finished. Now that he knew she would arrive in a few minutes, he fought the urge to run back to his hotel and allow Trey to handle the situation.

But Mason Walker had never backed down from a challenge in his life, and no way would he run off like a beaten dog with his tail between his legs.

After all, he wasn't the one who had failed to show up that day ten years ago.

He looked at the boy and forced another smile as he adjusted the bandage on his bad knee. "Your mom's on the way, Kid."

Sam seemed more interested in the pair of squirrels playing chase a few yards away. For a moment, Mason entertained the hope that their time together might be spent in silence. The last thing he needed to do right now was to play nice and hold any sort of conversation with Blair Montgomery's kid.

"Probably breaking the sound barrier to get here, huh?"

Sam finally said when the furry pair disappeared into a clump of trees.

"She did sound a little worried."

"Yeah, she worries about me a lot." He gave Mason a serious look. "She says it's 'cause she loves me so much, but ya know what?"

"What?" Mason shifted positions, trying in vain to get comfortable on the rock-hard ground.

"Sometimes I wish she didn't love me so much. I'd get to have a lot more fun."

"Don't ever wish your mom doesn't love you," he said, his voice sharper than he intended. He took a deep breath and let it out slowly. "But, hey, I know what you mean. Sometimes moms don't know what it's like to be a guy."

"I guess." Sam leaned back against the rough trunk of the ancient oak tree and pressed the ice pack to the left side of his face. His gaze landed on the bandage encircling Mason's knee. "What happened to you?"

"A big old catcher named Rock thought I shouldn't score the winning run while he was guarding home."

"Did ya?"

This time Mason's smile was genuine. "Yep."

Sam reached over and touched the bandage. "Does it hurt?" He shook his head. "It's nothing."

Actually it did, but he would never admit it. The dumb stunt he'd pulled last night had nearly been his undoing, and only by the force of sheer determination had he made it out of bed this morning.

He looked at the little guy next to him. Blair had a great kid, a real ballplayer. Not once had the boy complained about that lump he'd acquired. Even though he had been knocked flat by the pitch, he'd still managed to get up and run the bases.

He'd even stolen third and slid into home head first. Mason smiled. Sam reminded him of himself at that age. To shake the dismal feeling tagging alongside that thought, he snagged Sam's hat, pretended to juggle it, then set it on his head backward.

A pair of dimples flashed as the boy burst into a fit of giggles. Then he asked, "How'd you get the name Wild Man?"

He tried hard to think of a way to steer the conversation away from the name he'd acquired during the first hard year after Blair dumped him—a name that had followed him far longer than he deemed necessary. "How about if we talk about your nickname instead?"

Sam looked up at him with big blue eyes, his mother's eyes, Mason thought as he felt his heart lurch. He had spent hours staring into eyes just like those. Quickly, he pushed the memories away.

"I don't have a nickname," the boy said.

"Then we'll have to do something about that, won't we?" He ruffled the boy's straw-colored hair. "Tell me about yourself, and I'll see if I can think of a name for you."

"Cool!" he said, his eyes brightening with interest. "What d'ya wanna know?"

"Everything," Mason answered with a casualness he didn't feel. "Tell me about your mom and dad, school, what you like and don't like, stuff like that."

"Okay, let's see. My mom's pretty cool. She plants flowers for people. That's her job. Sometimes when I don't have school she lets me come along and help." He paused as if he were considering something important. "She gets real mad at Bubba when he gets in the way, so he doesn't get to go with us anymore."

"Is Bubba your brother?" The question sent Sam into peals of laughter. "What?" Mason asked.

"Bubba's my dog," he said through the giggles.

Mason thought back to the image of Sam and the mutt in the window. If Sam were his son, he'd have a proper dog, something manly like a Labrador retriever or a German shepherd. Definitely not a big dust mop with legs.

And he sure wouldn't be named Bubba.

"Well, do you have any brothers and sisters?" Mason asked.

"Nope. Just me and my mom."

"And your dad?" He knew he shouldn't care about the answer to that question, but he found himself holding his breath until the boy finally spoke.

"Nope. Just me and my mom," he repeated. "My dad's in heaven."

Mason felt himself breathe again, instantly ashamed at the wave of relief that washed over him. Blair was a free agent, just as Trey had claimed.

But why should this fact interest him? It had been too long ago. Why should he care?

Because he couldn't help himself. He corralled his wandering thoughts and focused on the conversation.

"My dad's with Jesus too," Mason managed to answer. "I miss him." And he did, especially when he put on that uniform and stepped onto the field.

"I never met mine," Sam said matter-of-factly. "He died before I was born."

Mason felt as if he'd been punched in the gut. Why hadn't he kept his mouth shut and not stuck his nose into Blair's business? Now he knew way too much.

Another thought struck him. This boy was at least eight years old, maybe nine. Blair had been a widow a long time. Why hadn't she contacted him in all these years?

Because she'd forgotten all about you by then, Man. You were ancient history, a blast from the past.

He shook his head and looked away rather than see himself reflected in those blue eyes. "So your mom took care of you by herself?" he finally managed to say.

"Nope."

"No?"

"Grandma Lettie lived with us until she died; then it was just us."

"Oh?" Mason didn't know whether to be relieved or more irritated. With Lettie James in charge, it was no wonder he'd never even rated as much as a Christmas card from Blair and her cozy little family.

"How long has your grandmother been gone?" Mason asked, not sure why he cared but unwilling to let the silence lengthen. Maybe talking about the demise of the geriatric terrorist might make him feel better, although he knew he'd have to make things right with the Lord on that score later on.

"Grandma Lettie died right before Christmas," he said, wiggling his sneaker-clad feet in time to some imaginary tune. "After that I got to plant flowers with Mom except when I'm at school." He screwed his face into a grimace; then, as quickly as it had come, the expression faded back to seriousness. "I like it better than school, but Mom says I have to go. But I'm a big help, and it's fun mostly."

"Oh, yeah?" The question was automatic, barely a grunt.

"Yeah. I liked it better than staying home with Grandma Lettie 'cause Mom lets me play in the dirt. Grandma Lettie used to say my daddy was always rolling around in the dirt and playing games even though he was a grown-up and shouldn't be doing stuff like that." He gave Mason a thoughtful look. "I don't think she liked him much."

Time to steer this conversation out of dangerous waters.

Again.

He searched for a more benign topic. "Let's get back to making up that nickname for you." He pretended to think, although he couldn't have strung two coherent thoughts together at gunpoint. "So, Buddy, there's bound to be something special for your name. When's your birthday?"

"It's coming up real soon."

Mason looked away. "Oh, yeah?"

"Yeah, it's August second. My mom says since I'm gonna be ten she's gonna take me and the guys to a ball game." Sam tossed the ice pack onto the grass. "This isn't cold anymore."

"Okay, I'll get you another one."

Mason rolled over on all fours and eased himself into a standing position, holding onto the tree trunk for support with one hand, the ice bag in the other.

A thought struck him, the force of it sending him reeling backward against the tree. Mason did the math.

Sam was his son. He had to be. And he was born the same day he and Blair were to meet at Luigi's. But why hadn't Blair told him about the baby she was carrying?

He said something, he must have, for he heard Sam answer, but his brain failed to register the words. Somehow he began to walk, putting one foot in front of the other until he found himself leaning against the burning hot hood of his Jeep in the parking lot.

"Ouch!"

Mason jumped away from the vehicle, slapping the warm bag onto the pain in his arm. It did nothing to dull the burn, but the action temporarily took his mind off the bigger ache that threatened to consume him.

He turned around and examined his face in the dark-tinted side window of the Jeep. No, he still looked the same.

And yet everything about him was different. All he believed to be true about himself had suddenly become skewed. Removing his ball cap, he ran his hand through his hair and pondered the situation.

He was a father.

Somehow he'd given life to a boy he never knew existed. For some reason Blair had judged him unfit for the task of being a father to her son. He banged the ice bag against the side of his leg.

But why? For the life of him he still had no answer.

"Hey, Walker! How's the kid?"

The familiar voice jarred his shattered nerves, jerking him back to the present with alarming speed. Twenty yards away, Trey stood waiting for an answer.

"He's fine." Mason hoped he sounded at least vaguely like his normal self as he returned the cap to his head.

Affecting a casual demeanor, he waved the lukewarm ice bag in the air. The last thing he needed to do right then was to try to explain something to Trey that he didn't understand himself.

"Need more ice." He turned away before his buddy could comment.

After he refilled the bag, Mason headed back to wait with Sam for Blair's arrival. As he stepped into the clearing between the snack bar and the stand of oaks and pines that ringed the park, he knew she was already there. He could feel her presence, just like the old days.

And, like the old days, her presence unnerved him. Squaring his shoulders, he plastered a smile on his face and walked toward the spot where he knew he'd find her. *Okay, Lord, walk me through this.*

"Sweetie," he heard her say, "are you sure you're all right? Maybe I need to call Dr. Fraser."

The familiar voice, in the soft tones he remembered all too well, tore at his composure. He felt his breath catch in his throat as he rounded the corner and glimpsed her.

"Aw, Mom, I'm fine," he heard Sam answer.

Frozen in place, Mason felt as if he stared heaven in the face. If anything, the years had been more than kind to Blair, something he hadn't noticed yesterday afternoon at the ballpark or last night in the dim light of her front yard.

But this was no angel, he reminded himself. This was the woman who'd taken his heart and trampled on it, leaving without so much as a backward glance.

"Blair."

When she looked his way, he knew he'd said it aloud. Eyes of rich azure blue widened, then closed, only to open again.

"Mason?"

Had she really said his name, or did he only imagine it?

Mason took a few halting steps toward her. The smile she gave him seemed genuine, if not a little slow in coming. When he returned it, all the hurt and most of the years melted away. He forced himself not to sprint the rest of the distance between them.

But that would mean he cared, that he was anxious to see her, speak to her. That couldn't be it.

"D'you two know each other?"

Sam's voice sliced through his mind, reminding him of what Blair had done to him. As quickly as they had fallen, the barriers went up again around his heart. He knew his smile had disappeared so he hastily looked away, making sure the face that returned to her was as impassive as he could make it.

He opened his mouth to speak, but the words seemed locked in his throat. Instead he turned his attention to the boy. Dimples flashing, Sam eyed the two of them with youthful wonder. Blair looked more than uncomfortable.

"Well, do ya?" Sam repeated.

"Yeah," Mason answered, trying to keep the trembling he felt out of his voice. "Your mom and I go way back."

three

He knew.

That's all Blair could think of as she watched Mason ease down into the combination of daylight and shadows. She eyed him critically through the dappled sunlight, watching for the slightest indication. His demeanor was friendly, to be sure, but there was something else. Recognition of some kind, she thought on first glance.

But as quickly as it appeared, it was gone. No, she decided, he had no idea the boy sitting next to him was his child. She relaxed, but only slightly. If he knew she'd seen him yesterday, he must wonder why she hadn't spoken to him. What possible reason could she give for beating a hasty retreat at the first sight of her former husband?

Mason's gaze traveled lightly over her to rest more intently on Sam. He ruffled the boy's hair and winked at him, as if sharing some sort of male-only secret. Blair looked away, unable to stomach the closeness she perceived between the two of them.

She'd gone to such lengths to keep them from meeting, and yet here they were, acting more like the father and son they were than the strangers they should have been. Fear once again rose in a tight knot in her chest. She shoved her hands into her pockets to keep them from shaking. Only her casual behavior could keep Mason from suspecting the obvious.

Dark hair mingled with light as Mason leaned down and whispered something in Sam's ear. Two sets of eyes the color of faded denim gazed in her direction. *How could Mason not know,* she thought as she watched them together? How could

28

he not see so much of himself in his son?

Sam's childish laughter bubbled with innocence as he leaned against the ample shoulder of the man who had given him life. Once again, their hair mingled in a pattern of light and dark that captured her attention and held it. Mason made a feeble attempt to keep a straight face, his arm wrapped around his son as he playfully jabbed him with his elbow.

"What?" The word sounded more like a croak than a question, and Blair instantly regretted having spoken.

"Mr. Wild Man said this is the first time he's ever seen you so quiet," Sam said, taking Mason's good-natured rough housing in stride.

She pulled her hands out of her pockets and smoothed a strand of hair behind her ear. "People change."

"But not you, Blair," Mason said softly.

"Look, Mason, about yesterday." She forced herself to look, really look, into his eyes. What she saw there revealed nothing, so she pressed on with her apology. "I was incredibly rude. I wasn't sure you saw me, but to leave like that—forgive me?"

"Forgive you?" He smiled, then let the corners of his mouth fall and shrugged. "Sure."

He had seen her. Well, the last thing she needed was for Mason to be angry. Better she smooth things out than leave him with any memory of her when he left to rejoin his team.

She frowned. How had he managed to get even one day off, much less the rest of the week? Had something happened?

"Don't you have to play. . . ?" Her voice trailed off. She noticed the bandage on his knee. "Oh, you're hurt."

His big, sturdy hand reached down to touch the wrappings on his knee. "It's nothing," he said.

"He did it running into home," Sam said, a note of authority in his voice. "You should have seen how many guys it took to carry old Rock off the field afterward."

She raised an eyebrow. "Oh, really?"

"Yep," Sam said with a nod. "But that's nothing compared to the time he got hit by a pitch." His gaze swung to Mason, a look of admiration on his face. "I heard all about it when they did that special on you for the Sports Channel. It was cool. You really made him pay, didn't ya, Wild Man?"

Mason looked uncomfortable. "Well, that was another time in my life, before the Lord and I. . ." His voice trailed off as he seemed to be searching for an appropriate answer.

Pulling off the blue ball cap, he ran his hand through his hair in an unconscious ritual she'd seen Sam perform hundreds of times. It broke Blair's heart that something so simple, a gesture done so many times it had most likely become mindless, could affect her so strongly. But everything about Mason Walker had affected her back then.

She stole another look and had to admit it still did. Sam tugged on her arm, bringing her thoughts crashing back to the present

"Tell Mom like you told me," he implored Mason.

&

Mason grimaced as he returned his cap to his head. The boy wouldn't rest until he thought of something to say. And from the look on his mother's face she was none too pleased.

Given his current state of mind, Mason could have cared less about Blair's feelings of discomfort. What he did care about, however, was making sure Sam understood. The last thing he wanted to do was give a false impression of what was right to the boy.

To his son.

His thoughts caught on the word and held there until Sam jarred him back to reality with a gentle poke in the ribs. "Hey, something wrong, Mr. Wild Man? You look sad."

"Naw, I'm fine," he said lightly. "It's just that I don't like talking about that stuff. I was a stupid, hot-headed player who did a whole lot of things wrong before Jesus Christ and

I paired up. I hardly think your mom's interested in my old war stories."

He picked up the ice bag, weighing it in his hand as he risked another peek at Blair. No smile seemed forthcoming. Quickly, he cast about for another subject. "How's that bump anyway?"

"It don't hurt much, I guess."

"It doesn't hurt much," Blair corrected.

"Yeah, that's what I said." Sam rubbed one grubby finger against the blue-black knot on his freckled cheek and looked up at his mother. "Do I get spaghetti for supper?"

Tilting the corners of her mouth into a wry smile, Blair gave the boy a sideways look.

"Sometimes when I get hurt or have a bad day, she tells me she'll make spaghetti for supper," Sam continued. "I bet your mom used to do the same thing, huh?"

No, but someone else I loved did.

He felt a tug on the sleeve of his shirt. "You're gonna have spaghetti with us, aren't you, Mr. Wild Man?"

Mason didn't miss Blair's sharp intake of breath. "Well, I'd like to, but—"

"I'm sure Mr. Walker already has plans for the evening." A thread of what sounded like panic rose in her voice.

Actually, he did have plans. He planned to fall into bed the minute he hit the empty hotel suite.

But no way would he tell them that.

"C'mon, Mr. Wild Man," Sam said. "My mom makes the best spaghetti in the whole world." He gave Mason a broad smile, with dimples appearing on either side of his mouth. "She'll even pick out the mushrooms if you don't like 'em."

"Sweetheart, Mr. Walker's a busy man. He probably has a plane to catch."

The boy's mother gazed at him expectantly, looking as if she knew he would agree. Mason smiled back and considered how much he would enjoy bursting Blair's bubble and letting her know he'd cashed in his ticket home and planned to stick around awhile.

At least until he could unravel the mystery of instant fatherhood.

"Spaghetti with no mushrooms." He pretended to contemplate the offer, allowing a small bit of joy at Sam's enthusiasm. "Now that's an offer I don't get very often."

"Aw, Mr. Wild Man, just say you're gonna come over," Sam said, the bump obviously forgotten. "We eat at six every day, and if you're late you don't get anything 'cept a peanut butter sandwich. Isn't that right, Mom?"

"That's right, Sam, but—"

"You gotta get all clean too. Mom's real funny about that. And don't wear your hat at the table, either. Mom says it's not polite."

He grudgingly admired the fact Blair cared enough about the boy to set some boundaries and stick by them. It said something about her and the kind of person she intended Sam to be. Unfortunately, the merit paled in comparison to the fact she'd chosen not to share this child with him.

"Please?"

The excitement in Sam's voice was contagious. If only the circumstances had been different.

How would he manage to get through an evening with the two of them? One look at Sam and he knew he'd have to try. "I'll come on one condition," he said, avoiding Blair's steady gaze. "You've got to stop calling me Wild Man."

"But—"

"No buts. Just call me Mason—deal?" He stuck out a hand to shake on it. *And maybe someday you'll call me Dad.*

"Deal!" The boy's pint-sized fingers easily disappeared in Mason's grasp. He was careful not to crush them. Too soon the manly gesture ended, the first agreement struck between father and son.

Mason slid a glance in Blair's direction. To his surprise, she gave him a shy smile.

"So dinner's at six?"

Her smile fell for a split second before she caught it. "It looks that way. Let me give you directions to my house." Blair pulled a small notebook from her purse and scribbled a few lines, then tore out the sheet and handed it to Mason. Without meeting Mason's gaze, she gathered her purse and stood, offering her hand to Sam. "Feel up to a trip to the grocery store, Slugger?"

Mason struggled to his feet. "You talking to him or me?" *Where did that come from?*

Her blue eyes widened in shock as a lovely shade of pink crept into her lightly freckled cheeks. "Well, actually—"

"Sorry, Ma'am," he said in his best John Wayne voice, arms outstretched. "Sam here says you're awful particular about having clean diners at your table, and right now I don't exactly qualify."

His poor imitation of a cowboy made her laugh, as it always had. Even in the worst of times it seemed he could make her laugh. Somehow he felt that talent might come in handy in the evening ahead. Despite the smile on her face, he had the distinct feeling she hadn't been thrilled he'd accepted the invitation.

But by the time he arrived at the white frame cottage on Whitley Road, freshly shaved and showered and bearing a bouquet of yellow roses, he'd concluded he didn't care how Blair reacted to his presence.

He stepped out of the Jeep, prayed up and determined not to leave this countrified version of Beaver Cleaver's neighborhood until he had the answers he wanted from her. The answers he deserved. She could start by telling him why she'd left without a trace in spite of their promise and finish up with a decent explanation of why she'd seen fit not to tell him of his impending fatherhood. And he wouldn't go anywhere until she did.

He strode past the white picket fence that surrounded the tiny yard, barely noticing the group of pint-sized ragamuffins clustered around the blue and white mailbox.

"Hey, M–mister, are you really Wild Man W–walker?" a squeaky voice called, halting his progress in mid-stride.

Mason turned slowly and came face-to-face with a band of kids that numbered almost a half dozen. Armed with various pieces of baseball equipment, they stared expectantly as their spokesman stepped forward and offered a pudgy hand.

"Pleased to meet you, Big Guy." Mason stifled a smile as he shook the boy's hand. Instantly, his mood improved. "Mason Walker."

A couple of the children elbowed each other, exchanging glances and quiet murmurs before growing silent again. Mason leaned down and smiled at the little fellow. "How can I help you?"

"W–well, see, we heard you might be in the neighborhood, so we th–thought it would be all right"—he colored a bright red as one of his friends poked him from behind—"you see, we really like b–baseball, and we were wondering—"

The Lord knew how much Mason loved children. They were some of the last honest folks left on the planet. He should've had a house full of them to come home to instead of an expensive but empty condo in Waikiki.

He shook his head. Baseball had been good to him. Why would he want to do anything else? His attention returned to the squirming boy. "Whatcha got there?"

"A g–glove."

"Nice glove." He lifted it out of the boy's outstretched hand. "But there's something wrong with it."

Brown eyes widened. "What?"

"Here—take these flowers and let me have a closer look."

Mason handed him the roses and pretended to study the well-worn leather a moment, turning it over as he ran his hand over the names that covered its surface. "This has a couple of pretty good ballplayers' autographs on it."

The boy's chest swelled, and he clutched at the lump of flowers, effectively smashing a good portion of the yellow blooms. "Yep. My daddy took me and Sam to see the Astros play last summer, and I got those autographs there. I'm gonna get some more next time we go."

"What's your name?"

"Brian McMinn." A couple of others snickered, and the boy frowned at them before turning back to Mason. "I live right there." He pointed to the house next door. "Me and Sam are best friends."

"Well, Brian, I'll tell you what's wrong with this glove. It's missing my autograph." He lowered his voice and leaned closer to the astonished boy. "I'd be real honored if you'd let me sign my name right here next to that pitcher of theirs. If I remember right, he's the guy who pitched to me when I hit my first big-league home run."

He took the pen offered him and signed his name next to the scribbled signature of the overpaid player who'd almost taken his head off the last time he'd met him on the ball field. The round of *oohs* and *ahhs* that followed made him all but forget the prima donna pitcher.

Mason handed the glove back to the beaming child. "Thanks. That was a real honor. Anyone else have something they want signed?"

As the rest of the group elbowed for position, he settled on an old painted bench in the shade of a towering oak, leaning his back against its crackled surface. He heard the screen door slam, then Sam's voice as the boy bounded toward them.

"Mr. Wild Man! I mean, Mason!" he shouted. "You're here!" He hugged Mason, then settled down beside him on the bench.

The aroma of garlic and tangy marinara sauce wafted toward Mason on the warm evening breeze as he spent the next half hour talking baseball and signing autographs. Through it all, Sam never gave up his place at Mason's side. When the screen door opened again, he knew it had to be Blair, and he stood to greet her with a promise to the youngsters that he'd be back another day.

The small group dispersed, leaving him alone with Blair and Sam. He looked around, taking in the scenery with a smile.

"I see you still have a way with flowers." He ran his hand over the red and white blooms that spilled out of a hanging basket beneath an ancient oak tree. "Best I remember, your mom could make anything grow," he said to Sam, who trailed behind him as he moved toward the house.

Too soon, Mason reached the porch and Blair. Reminding himself that he was a man on a mission, not a guy on a date, he steeled himself for the encounter, offering her the flowers instead of his hand.

Dressed in a flowing creation of yellow a shade lighter than the roses, she looked as if someone had taken sunshine and wrapped her in it. She accepted the flowers and murmured a word of thanks. Instantly, he resented her for looking so good.

He frowned, not caring that she saw. It would make his job tonight that much tougher if he allowed himself to be distracted.

Lord, let me remember I'm here for Sam. Grant me the strength to do what's right for him.

Still he allowed himself the luxury of one long look, starting with the burnished gold of her hair, this time worn away from her face, a barrette capturing the honeyed strands. The modest cotton dress she'd chosen was perfect, its soft yellow fabric sprigged with tiny blue flowers that matched the color of her eyes.

How many times had those eyes appeared in his dreams, overflowing with tears as she begged him to marry her all over again?

The answer was simple. Too many.

He continued his lazy perusal of her appearance, sure he was in complete control of his emotions. Just a man on a mission.

She spoke, and his concentration shattered. "Go wash for dinner, Sam," she said, watching the boy disappear inside the house before turning her attention to Mason. "Sam's thrilled you could make it."

He could tell she was nervous, and this pleased him. "And you?" Mason spoke before he realized what had happened, the words falling from his lips like the traitorous things they were.

Mason mentally condemned his stupidity. The first thing he said to her, and it came out sounding as if he cared what she thought of him. Which was ridiculous, he reminded himself, because he didn't care. Really, he didn't. He was just a man on a mission.

Only the opinion of the Lord and his son mattered. Blair was merely someone from his past.

"I'm glad too, Mason." Her voice wrapped around his name and caressed it like a breeze from heaven. "It's been a long time."

Too long. Not that he cared, because he didn't.

Resting one foot on the wide wooden boards of the porch, he leaned against the rail and clutched it with both hands like a lifeline. For a moment, neither of them spoke.

A car passed on the road, kicking up a whirlwind of dust. Still no words were exchanged.

He dared himself to look into her eyes, risking he would feel nothing. He lost.

And when he lost, he lost himself as well. But at the same time he found the part of his soul he had been missing all those years. She had stolen it, taken it long ago without asking.

Sadly, she probably never knew she had it. Even worse, he realized he didn't want it back.

"Whatcha doing' out on the porch? I'm starving in here." Sam stared at him through the screen door.

From where Mason stood, he could tell the boy had combed his hair and changed into a clean shirt. He felt suitably impressed.

Blair moved first, pushing past the barriers his heart had erected, to disappear inside the little frame house. Reluctantly he followed, knowing his mission had fallen sadly into danger.

four

Lord, guide my steps, Mason prayed.

Ignoring the pounding of his heart, he stepped inside the cottage. The room unfolded before him, and he felt his world tilt. Nothing in all his imaginings had prepared him for this.

Scattered throughout were touches of a life he thought he'd forgotten. A wild array of flowers in a simple glass jar stood on a little wooden table that had adorned their own tiny living room. In the corner by the window, the brass floor lamp they'd found in a little junk store in East Texas provided a subdued golden light. The lamp had been their first acquisition after the wedding, bought when thirty dollars was a lot of money and the rest of their lives still lay ahead of them.

He crossed the wide-plank oak floor, losing himself in the memories. A leather-bound book about New England gardens he'd purchased for her on a rare trip back home leaned against a container. He moved the book out of the way and picked up the container, a jelly jar he'd filled with bluebonnets and presented to her.

Smiling to himself, he thought about how he'd almost been gored by an old bull when he was picking those flowers. Blair had given him a hard time about that, even though he'd ended up with only a broken nose and a few scratches. Somehow he had known she was pleased he'd cared enough to risk life and limb over a bunch of blue flowers.

After all, they were her favorite. He wondered if she liked them because they matched her eyes.

He paused and savored the moment, remembering all this and more. Then, as quickly as it appeared, his smile faded. As great as things had been, as much as he'd loved her, it hadn't been enough. His love hadn't kept her with him. It hadn't made her stay.

To be fair, they were both guilty, he realized with a start. Each had followed their dreams, even if it seemed as though he had been the only one who'd paid the price in loneliness.

The warm memories turned cold, following the course of his thoughts to the day he learned she'd married someone else.

He could remember every detail, every moment of that day with a clarity that surpassed even his wedding day and his first big league game.

"Done anything dangerous lately?"

Blair's gentle voice jarred him back to the present. He replaced the jelly jar on the shelf before turning to face her. "I'm here, aren't I?"

She stepped into the glow of the lamp, her clean, floral perfume preceding her. He could count every freckle on her nose; yet, despite the hardness in his heart, she wasn't standing nearly as close as he wished.

"Yes, you are."

Her wistful tone caught him off guard, stabbing him with the slightest feeling of guilt for his anger. She seemed to recover quickly, and he wondered if he'd imagined it.

"Are those hands clean?" she asked playfully.

He held them out for her inspection, hoping she would touch them, take them, and close the distance between them, anything but just stand there looking so beautiful. Then she gave him a little half smile, and he sensed she must feel as uncomfortable as he did.

Good.

"Then let's eat." She looked away.

He nodded and offered her his arm, hoping she wouldn't take it and praying she would. When her fingers touched his bare arm just inside the elbow, he felt as if he'd been hit in the stomach by a ninety-mile-an-hour fast ball.

Neither of them moved for what seemed like an eternity.

"Why?" Mason formed the question, giving voice to it before reason forbade it, yet speaking it so quietly he doubted he'd made a sound. Her grip tightened, and he knew she'd heard. He forced himself to look into her eyes and saw them cloud with some unnamed emotion. Somewhere in the house, a clock struck six times. "Blair, why?"

Again it was more of a breath than a question. Her dark, thick lashes flew up at the sound of her name. His hand moved to touch her cheek, running his finger across the smooth line of her jaw. Still she stood frozen, eyes closed.

"You two comin', or do I hafta eat all by myself?" a childish voice called.

"I guess that's our cue," Blair said unevenly, not looking at him. She broke away from his touch and disappeared down the hall leading away from the front door.

Mason caught up with her as she stepped into an airy, old-fashioned kitchen that spanned the rear of the house. At one time the room must have been a porch of some sort, Mason decided, as he followed Blair and watched her place the roses on the dark-blue ceramic counter top. A high, wooden ceiling loomed over brilliant white cabinets, while a half-dozen hanging plants filled windows behind them. Several copper pots bubbled on the ancient porcelain monstrosity that passed for a stove, their fragrant contents beckoning him forward as Blair removed a loaf of bread from the oven.

He was watching her close the oven door when something caught his attention out the window behind her. Past a broken swing set, he saw a profusion of flowers and Sam's dog sleeping happily in the midst of them. Under other circumstances, he might have laughed.

"May I do anything?" he asked instead.

"You could put the roses in water." She pulled a large bowl

of green salad out of the refrigerator. "There's a vase about the right size under the sink."

Their gazes held for a moment over the salad bowl. Blair opened her mouth to speak, then, apparently thinking better of it, carried the blue and white container to the table without uttering a word.

Shuffling through the contents under the sink, he finally came upon a rather decrepit-looking green vase. He held it up, fairly certain it hadn't seen use in years. "Don't get a lot of flowers, do you, Blair?"

"Nope." Her voice softened, fading to a murmur as she set the table. "Mine usually come from the yard, and it's generally Sam bringing them to me."

He shoved the flowers into the water and tried not to think of anything but the reason he was standing at her sink.

Watching her under the curtain of his lashes, he felt a familiar stab of emotion. Folding napkins and placing them on the table, Blair obviously had no idea of the picture of domestic happiness she presented to him.

He blinked, focusing his attention on the dark green vase in front of him.

Set the flowers on the counter.

Look out the window.

Do any of a hundred meaningless things to take your mind off her. Just don't let her get to you. Don't fall in love again.

No, he definitely would not fall in love with her again. He couldn't. He'd come tonight only to find out why.

As Sam came bounding into the room, another thought occurred to Mason. Maybe he was also here to get to know his son. He had nearly ten years to make up for, after all. Tomorrow he would get in touch with his lawyer and see what his rights were.

But first he had to get through tonight.

He offered her what he hoped would be a broad smile and

placed the vase on the counter next to a red-white-and-blue trivet in the shape of a star. He guessed Sam must have made it because it was lopsided.

"Is there anything else I can do?" he asked.

"Just have a seat," she answered, slipping the crusty bread into a basket. "I hope you don't mind, but Sam and I usually dine informally."

"Of course not. You're talking to a guy who eats the bulk of his meals in a stadium."

Mason eased onto the closest chair, his mind still on that stolen afternoon. He swallowed hard and hoped the direction of his thoughts didn't show on his face.

Amazing, but his memory was a fickle thing. Whole years of his life had gone by without anything special to remember in them; yet every moment of their four-week marriage stood out in his mind as if it were yesterday. He shifted in his chair.

Blair and Sam began filling their plates. Pushing the memories away, he followed suit with a casualness he didn't feel. Sam jabbed a skinny elbow into Mason's ribs.

"Wanna say the blessing?" he whispered.

He winked at Sam to cover his surprise. "Why don't you do the honors, Sport?"

He felt Sam grasp his hand tightly. "Thank You, Lord, for Mom's good food and for bringing Mason here tonight," the boy said. "I like him a lot. Amen."

Mason returned the squeeze. "And I like you a lot too, Sam. Thanks for inviting me."

While being in Blair's presence felt unsettling to say the least, spending time with the boy had proved to be nothing short of delightful. He found himself craving more of it. "Maybe we can get together before I have to leave. Maybe hit the batting cages or grab some burgers," Mason said casually. "Would you like that?"

"Would I?" Sam paused and turned to his mother. "If it's okay with you, Mom."

⁊a

"When do you leave?" Blair said quickly. A little too quickly, she decided, masking her embarrassment by taking a long drink of water.

"I won't know until tomorrow."

"Oh?" As much as she wanted him to disappear, the thought of his leaving bothered her more than she cared to admit. She took another sip.

"Yeah, I have an MRI scheduled for tomorrow morning. What they find will determine when I play again."

"Oh."

Blair took a bite of spaghetti, surprised to find it had no taste. So he didn't plan a swift exit. She tried hard to pin down exactly how she felt about that, an impossible task given the fact that the object of those mixed feelings sat across the table from her.

"You sound disappointed."

Somehow she swallowed the bite. "No, it's not that. I mean, I'm just surprised—that's all. I thought you would have to wait until it stopped hurting to play again."

"If I wait for that to happen, I may as well quit." He took a bite of salad, washing it down with the rest of his water.

Praying for a steady hand, she reached for the pitcher and refilled his glass. "You mean you'd play hurt?"

As quickly as the words were spoken, Blair wished she could reel them back in. The Mason Walker she'd known so long ago would have played baseball even if he had to drag himself onto the field to do it.

And she had seen him do just that more than a few times.

She hated the memory and wished for some magic words to erase everything related to Mason from her mind. Sadly, she knew nothing short of a miracle would accomplish the feat.

Too many years had passed, and she'd given up praying for that sort of miracle. Most of the time her prayers were for peace and understanding now.

"If the doc says I'm able to play, I play," he said without looking at her.

"Of course."

As Mason turned to speak to Sam, Blair took the opportunity to study him. The years had been good to him, she decided.

A little broader across the shoulders and slightly thicker through the arms, his powerful body could still fill a room with his presence. Brushed away from his face and trimmed to a length slightly below his collar, his gently waving dark hair was showing a few threads of silver at the temples. In the late afternoon sunlight, she realized it only made him more handsome.

He was dressed in a simple white polo shirt and a pair of jeans and still wore his good looks as if he had no idea he possessed them. A thin gold chain, his only jewelry besides a watch, glittered bright against the darkly tanned skin of his neck.

Nothing fancy about Mason Walker, she thought. But there never had been.

He looked in her direction and smiled, dimples flashing, and she felt her knees go weak. Gripping her glass, she took another sip of water and prayed for strength. Still, she couldn't look away.

Age lines crinkled on either side of his amazing blue eyes, fading with his grin as he turned to Sam to answer a question. He refilled his glass and swiveled back in her direction to pour her a generous portion as well.

She nodded, her mouth suddenly dry. "Thank you."

"You're welcome." His direct gaze shifted to Sam, then returned to her.

He picked up the blue-checked napkin and wiped at the corner of his mouth. Her gaze went from the rectangle of cloth in his hand to his eyes that studied her intently.

She wondered if he realized why she loved the color blue so much. *Probably not,* she thought, lowering her gaze to take another bite of the tasteless dinner before her.

Men never noticed things like that.

⋙

Halfway though the plate of spaghetti, Mason remembered why he never took his dates to Italian restaurants. Spaghetti made a mess.

He rubbed at the bright red spot on his jeans where a mound of sauce had landed and pretended an interest in the conversation swirling around him. While he watched the spot change to a dull orange, he caught snatches of a story about something Sam did as a baby. His attention piqued.

"Then Grandma told me if I was ever gonna learn how to walk I was gonna have to try harder so she took away my bottle and put it where I couldn't reach it. She said if I wanted it I had to go get it myself."

"He was almost eighteen months old," Blair explained, as if that fact had any relevance.

"So?" Mason's eyes went from the smiling boy to his mother.

"We were desperate." She gave him a look that told him she thought he should understand.

Well, he didn't. Instead his temper rose at the injustice his son had to endure at the hands of those women. He hadn't walked until long past the time he was supposed to, and he'd turned out fine, a fact he was about to point out to both of them when Sam elbowed him.

"Know what I did then?"

"Nope," he answered.

"I got so mad that I stood up and did it." He fairly beamed.

"I learned to walk all by myself."

Mason felt his chest swell with pride. "That's great, Buddy. You wanted that bottle, and you went for it."

"Nope." He stifled a giggle. "Not even close. Want to guess what I wanted?"

He glanced at Blair. She looked away.

"I give up. What?"

"Anyone want more salad?"

The high-pitched tone in Blair's voice caught him off guard. He noticed the deep pink on her cheeks as she stood and carried the salad bowl to the sink without waiting for an answer. A second later, she returned and began clearing the bread and marinara sauce off the table.

"Guess," Sam said.

Mason tore his attention away from Blair. "What?"

"Samuel Montgomery! That dog has flattened my geraniums again." Blair stood looking out the window, hands on her hips. "Do something with him!"

"Yes, Ma'am." Sam stuffed the last bite of bread in his mouth and washed it down with a swallow of milk. "It's probably 'cause of Melanie's cat again."

"I hardly think it's the cat's fault that your dog is sleeping in my flower bed." She gave Sam a long look. "And wipe your face. You're wearing half your dinner."

Mason discreetly covered the orange spot on his jeans with his napkin. He noted with dismay that the once-clean cloth now had a bright red stain that matched the one on Sam's chin. Covering it with his hand, he leaned back in his chair and observed the exchange between mother and son.

Sam shrugged. "Aw, he's just tired from watching after us all night." He swiped at the spaghetti sauce on his chin.

"I don't care," she said. "Remove him. Take him for a walk or something, but get him out of my garden."

He shot Mason a knowing look and smiled. "Yes, Ma'am."

Carrying his plate and glass to the sink, he pulled a bright red cap out of the back pocket of his faded denim shorts and placed it backward on his head. A thick shock of blond hair stuck out through the back of the cap and fell onto his forehead.

"I still get pie, right?" He gave his mother a determined look. "'Cause it's not my fault Bubba wants to protect us all the time. I told him he's got to be the man of the house when I'm not here."

Mason felt his heart sink. The man of the house should be someone besides a nine-year-old boy or a mutt.

He glanced in Blair's direction. She'd begun washing the dishes, ignoring him and Sam as her hands moved beneath the surface of the sudsy water.

"Yes, you'll still get pie." She looked up from her task. "Now scoot!"

Dropping the cloth onto the counter, she crossed to the table where she began to stack the remaining dishes. Out of the corner of his eye, Mason saw Sam heading for the door, a bright purple leash in his hand.

A thought occurred to him. "Hey, Pal. You never told me what made you want to walk so much," he said.

Sam smiled at him, his dimples dancing. With his free hand he opened the door, and his dog bolted onto the porch, then stopped and pranced back to his master's feet.

"A baseball." He leaned over and fastened the leash onto Bubba's collar. "Grandma put my bottle right next to it. Only she didn't know it was there 'cause Mom kept it in a little box with blue flowers on it and let me play with it only when it was just us at home." He shrugged. "I don't think Grandma liked baseball much. Hey, y'know, you never did think of a cool nickname for me."

Mason swallowed hard and hoped his voice still worked. "I didn't?" was all he could manage, and it came out sounding like a croak.

"Nope." The boy stood there while his dog ran in circles around his feet, tangling him in the leash. A pattern of muddy paw prints emerged as the dog slid and jumped about him.

"Well, I guess we'll have to work on that." Mason dropped his gaze to study the floor. "Now go take care of that mutt before your mom tells both of us we don't get pie."

He nodded and smiled broadly, then disappeared off the porch. A little piece of Mason's heart went with him. This time when he looked at Blair, she turned away. He knew without looking she had begun to cry.

Something moved him across the old linoleum tiles of the kitchen floor. When he wrapped his arms around her, all the hurt of the last ten years faded away.

She leaned back against his chest and wiped at her eyes with the dishtowel. "It was your—"

"First home run in the minors. I had to pay the guy who caught it ten bucks to get it back," he said, finishing her sentence.

"And it was the last ten bucks we had until the end of the week," she said quietly.

"I told you it would have to do for an engagement gift until I signed that ten-million-dollar contract and could afford a real wedding." He paused, holding her closer while losing his hold on his feelings. "I can't believe you kept it."

five

Blair couldn't believe she'd kept it, either.

Those memories and more came flooding back as she closed her eyes and allowed herself a moment to pretend it hadn't been ten years since he'd last held her like this.

Forgive him, Blair. Forgive him as I have forgiven you.

The dishtowel fell at her feet, and her eyelids slid open. She focused on the towel rather than the man, the situation rather than the words bouncing around in her head. The issue of forgiveness was best dealt with another time.

His fingers encircled her wrist. Imagine the idiocy of leaning into the embrace of the one man she'd made her life's mission to avoid. Where was her brain?

A moment later, she felt his finger lift her chin. In self-defense she closed her eyes.

"Blair, look at me."

Against her better judgment she did.

Was it a trick of the light, or had the years fallen away to reveal the Mason Walker to whom she'd pledged her love and her life all those years ago? She blinked hard, but the image of the young Mason, crooked smile and lock of unruly hair teasing his brow, remained.

Lord, please don't let me fall in love with him again.

The thought sobered her. Forgiveness she'd consider, but love was entirely out of the question. As was standing this close, dredging up these memories, entertaining these thoughts.

"Dessert?" she asked, knowing full well the change of topic was not a smooth one. "I have pie and—"

Then he kissed her, and she was nineteen years old and

speechless in his presence again. A girl unsure of herself and yet so sure Mason Walker was her whole world.

Her hands, of their own volition, found his shoulder and held on as he gently pulled away to touch her chin. He met her wavering gaze.

"I shouldn't have done that," he whispered.

Despite the legion of butterflies milling about in her stomach and the taste of marinara sauce on her lips, she somehow smiled. "No, you shouldn't have," she whispered back, although she couldn't think of a single reason why not.

Then he kissed her again. This time she threw out her cautious thoughts and dared to return the kiss.

Kissing Mason Walker brought up so many good memories. She reached for each precious moment as she reached for the back of Mason's neck and tangled her fingers in his hair. She held her memories to the light and relived each one in her mind, allowing the anger and distrust that had built up over the years to disappear. Forgiveness, that elusive decision she'd postponed so long, began to seem like an option.

Lord, what is happening?

The word forgiveness entwined with the word love and danced about in her mind until she forced them into submission. This was a kiss, nothing more; and if she wanted to kiss Mason Walker in the privacy of her own kitchen in broad daylight, then she could.

Just then the phone rang.

She ignored it. In fact, she wasn't sure she'd heard it. She knew Mason hadn't.

Then the phone rang again. This time the shattering sound broke the moment and their embrace.

"Phone," he whispered, raking a hand through his hair.

Her arms reached for him. "Answering machine," she said softly.

"Good."

A second later, the loud beep punctuated Blair's recorded request for the caller to leave a message. "Hello, Blair. I missed you today."

The distinct drawl carried easily through the quiet house, reminding Blair she hadn't called Griffin Davenport back to reschedule the meeting she'd missed because of Sam's accident.

Blair felt Mason tense beneath her touch. A fraction of a second later, he backed away.

"I'm up for tomorrow at noon if you still are," her client continued. "Just give me a call. You know the number."

Mason's eyes shut tight as the dial tone signaled the end of the message. In the span of half a minute, whatever feelings had passed between them seemed to slip away.

His eyes opened. "Hot date tomorrow?"

"Date? With Mr. Davenport?" She forced a chuckle. "Not hardly."

Mason looked away, apparently studying the table. "I have to get going."

"Mason, I—" She ran out of words and reached out to touch the back of his hand. Still he wouldn't look at her.

Instead, he cleared his throat and smiled faintly, his gaze now focused on some point behind her head. "Thank you for dinner. I'll tell Sam good-bye on my way out."

His footsteps echoed a swift rhythm on the hardwood floor; then the screen door slammed, and voices rose outside, along with the sound of a yapping dog. Sam's high, youthful tones mingled with Mason's deep voice until Blair couldn't stand to listen anymore.

She held her hands over her ears and willed herself to remember why he no longer had a place in her life.

Outside an engine cranked to a start, roaring in her ears along with the pounding of her heart. With all the dignity she could muster, she crossed the linoleum floor, her sandals making a loud slapping noise.

She walked toward the traitorous answering machine, punched the rewind button so hard the box fell off the table, then watched as the old black rotary phone crashed to the floor.

The dial tone shifted to a loud, angry beep. When a message from the phone company cordially warned her the phone was off the hook, she felt the first tear fall.

She gave the phone a good kick and went back to the kitchen to finish the dishes. On the counter a freshly bought apple pie from the best bakery in town mocked her. She fought the urge to throw the pie into the soapy water or, worse, to slice herself a huge chunk of it and drown it in vanilla ice cream.

Instead, she squared her shoulders, picked up the dishtowel from the floor, and headed for the sink and the pots and pans still decorating the counter.

"Oh!" She dabbed at her eyes impatiently. "Well, this was what you wanted. He's gone. Out of your life."

ã€‰

Speeding down the empty country roads, he wished for his favorite black Porsche instead of the slower, less responsive Jeep. More times than he could count, he'd slipped behind the wheel of that little car and outrun his torments, losing himself in the purr of the powerful engine and the strength of prayer until the reason for his troubles had been forgotten.

But the Porsche was back at his home in Honolulu, and he was here, running away from Magnolia, Tennessee, with his tail between his legs.

Despite his intentions to the contrary, his thoughts turned to Blair and the deep feelings she managed to evoke in him. Instantly, he pushed them away.

He reached for his cellular phone. Punching in the number for his attorney's office in Honolulu, he steered the vehicle onto the interstate and waited for the secretary to answer before putting him through to Mike Brighton.

"Mason, how wonderful to hear from you again. I've been meaning to call you."

Lisa. The sound of the junior partner's soft, feminine voice caught him off guard, and he almost rear-ended a slow-moving log truck. Quickly, he swerved and regained his composure. "I really need to speak to the boss man. It's important."

The last person he needed to talk to right now was the woman who'd arrived on his doorstep in Montana two weeks ago declaring her intentions to see to his recuperation personally and privately. Before her high-heeled shoes could touch the front porch, Mason had sent her packing.

"I'm sorry about that little scene up in Montana," she said sweetly. "I just assumed, what with you being such a man of the world, that my offer—"

"Never assume," Mason ground out. He pressed harder on the gas, and the Jeep lurched forward.

Lord, control my tongue and make my words edifying to You. Otherwise, I'm about to lose my temper.

He jerked the wheel to the left in time to pass a minivan loaded with kids and camping equipment, then slowed his speed as the highway became more congested.

"Look, Lisa—it's been real nice talking to you, but I need to speak to Michael pronto."

"Are you sure there's nothing I can help you with?"

He felt only revulsion. "Positive."

After a few parting words, she reluctantly surrendered him to the managing partner. When he heard the masculine voice on the line, he released his tight grip on the steering wheel.

"Mason, good to hear from you, my friend. What can I do for you?"

Briefly he told him about the situation with Blair and Sam. A long pause filled the air as Mason signaled to turn into the hotel parking lot.

"Are you certain?" the attorney asked.

He'd done the math, worked out all the angles. There was no other explanation. And yet what about the Davenport fellow? In his heart, he couldn't consider it. Unless proven otherwise, Mason had to believe Sam was his son.

"I'm positive, Mike."

"Okay. As your attorney and, more important, as your friend, I have to ask you this." He hesitated. "Are you absolutely certain she's not running a scam on you?"

Mason briefly allowed a replay of the kiss they'd shared. Kisses, he amended with a frown. Nothing to get worked up about. He'd have to do a better job of avoiding Blair in the future. "I was married to her once, okay?"

"Oh?"

"The divorce was final just over ten years ago." He paused. "Ten years, get it? That's how old Sam is." Again he hesitated. "She doesn't even know I've figured it out."

"All right then. We have the element of surprise in our favor."

"The element of surprise?" Mason shook his head. "You make it sound like a war, Mike."

"And well it might be. She's obviously gone to great lengths to hide this child from you. It sounds like things could get ugly if we go in unprepared."

"Ugly?" Again he remembered the touch of her lips against his. "No, that's not Blair's style." But was it? He had no idea.

"Fine then. I can only give you preliminary advice based on what you've told me so far. At this juncture, our first course of action is to establish the child's paternity through legal channels. The second step will be to determine your rights and decide whether to pursue custody arrangements. Do you have access to a birth certificate?"

"Nope," he said as he let off on the accelerator.

"Then we'll have to do it the hard way. Do you think the mother is amenable to having DNA testing done on the boy?

I could have the papers drawn up and faxed over in the morning. You could have your answer in record time."

Mason grimaced. She might not take kindly to his snooping around looking for proof that Sam was his son, especially if it involved lawyers and blood tests.

Besides, he would never have someone stick a needle in the boy just to prove he was his. Not if he could help it, anyway.

He also had to consider the possibility that Blair might run again. "Is there any other way?"

The attorney's hesitation lasted long enough for Mason to worry. "Nothing that won't take some time," he finally said.

"Time's something I don't have. I have an MRI tomorrow morning, and if that goes okay I could be leaving for a rehab assignment in a couple of days. I'd like to have proof before I go."

He heard the attorney let out a long breath. "Can you stall for time?"

"You have to be kidding."

"Okay, okay. It was a bad suggestion. Let me think of something. Where can I reach you later?"

"You have my cell number. I'll be at the hotel." Mason climbed out of the Jeep and tossed the keys to the valet.

An hour later, he leaned back in the chair in his hotel room and adjusted the bindings on his knee. Then, drumming on the newspaper in his lap, he sipped a glass of orange juice.

A little less painful this evening, his knee still felt stiff. The appointment tomorrow morning loomed large in his mind. He could guess what the outcome of the MRI would be, but what the Waves management would make of it was another thing altogether.

From experience, he knew his return to the team would have nothing to do with any medical tests. When the Waves needed him, they would find an expert to pronounce him fit to play, and he'd return.

He always did.

After all, playing baseball was his job, one that too many other guys would happily take away from him given the chance. Long ago he'd learned to accept the aches and pains and deal with them. A strong belief in the power of prayer had helped too.

He lifted the heavy glass to his lips. The doctor he'd privately consulted two years ago had warned him if he continued to play he might have permanent knee damage. He'd predicted Mason wouldn't finish the season before his knee gave out, then the guy had practically dared him to prove him wrong.

Well, Mason had shown them all. Not only had he finished that season, but he'd played a couple of more since. He shook his head. The Lord had blessed him with the ability to play ball; he needed to remember that.

He also thought about where he'd learned his work ethic. His unshakable belief in God hadn't taken root until well into his twenties. Before that, the only father he knew was a man whose love of the game superseded any feelings he had for his son.

Every time he swung the bat and watched the ball fly past the outfielder's head and into the bleachers, he thought about his earthly father and the endless tirades that accompanied his coaching, about the stern-faced doctor and his gloom-and-doom predictions. His dad's desire for perfection was something Mason had taken to heart, molding it into a character trait some called a character flaw. Yes, he'd listened to his father and learned never to quit.

For that reason, he'd ignored the doctor. He was a good medical man, the best out there, according to his sources. But when it came to Mason Walker and his desire to play the game of baseball, the guy didn't have a clue.

Just as Mason reached for the remote control, the sound of

his cell phone shattered the quiet in the room. He set what was left of his drink on the table and picked up the receiver on the second ring.

"Yes?"

"Mason, it's Michael Brighton again."

"Hey, Mike." He picked up a hotel pen from the table and began to scribble on the sports page. "What do you have for me?"

A long pause. Mason colored in a dark blue mustache over the latest contender for the Cy Young pitching award.

"Mike?"

"Sorry, Mason, but I've come up short. I'm going to need more time to get the goods on the woman and her son."

He took a deep breath and tried to remember that he and the lawyer were working on the same side. "Look—I never said anything about getting the goods on Blair. You know me better than that, Mike."

"I regret my unfortunate use of words. Let me rephrase. I'd like to hire a private investigator. Maybe he can get to the bottom of all this."

"No." Mason gripped the pen in his hand and heard it snap. "I don't want anyone snooping around Blair and Sam."

"Then what do you suggest I do?"

He pitched the remains of the broken hotel pen into the wastebasket. "I don't care what you do, Mike, but keep Blair out of this."

"Mason, she's already in this up to her eyeballs."

Ignoring the sarcasm in Brighton's voice, Mason concentrated his gaze on the sports page in his lap. "What is it you need to know?"

"I need something concrete to go on. A birth certificate with your name on it would be ideal. Why don't you see if you can find one in a baby book? Surely the woman keeps that sort of thing lying around. They often do."

"So you want me to waltz into her house and ask to look at the boy's baby book?" The thought of going back there chilled him.

Mason heard him let out a long breath. "I didn't tell you to ask."

The implication of the lawyer's statement hit him hard. "I can't do that." Mason studied the glass before him.

"Look, Mason—we've known each other what, seven, eight years?"

"Yep." He tossed the paper on the floor, picked up the glass, and held it to the light, examining it as if the act of inspection would somehow remove him from the conversation at hand.

"Yet in all these years you've never once mentioned this woman?"

"Yep." Mason replaced the glass on the table and thought of their kiss, albeit one inspired by temporary insanity. He picked up the newspaper again and retrieved another pen from the desk drawer to continue drawing on the paper.

"I don't understand."

Mason said a quick prayer for guidance before speaking his mind. "I know Sam is mine, Mike. A father"—he tested the word on his tongue—"a father knows his son. I want him to know me too."

The silence was deafening. "What exactly do you want?"

"I want something permanent. I'm afraid she's going to bolt again, Mike, and it'll be another decade before I see my son. I need to be sure that doesn't happen. Legally, I mean."

"Okay." To his credit Mike's reply was soft, almost emotional, and out of character for the man Mason knew.

"I realize that before I go to Blair with this I need to have proof, and I don't think she's going to give me proof willingly. Now, within the bounds of reason, what do you suggest?"

Mason finished his artwork on the Cy Young candidate, then allowed the newspaper to fall to the floor.

"How do you feel about spending more time with the woman?"

How did he feel about it? Scared to death, that's how he felt about it.

He'd walked into her house a man on a mission and left a man on the run. That thought alone made him feel like a fool. Now his lawyer wanted him to step back into the spider's web?

"I'll manage," he said as he hung up the phone, not really sure he would.

≥

June 22

Blair put away the last of the breakfast dishes and contemplated the spot where she'd stood last night. In Mason's arms she'd forgotten everything she'd promised herself ten years ago. Involuntarily, she touched her lips with her finger, remembering their kiss.

She should never have let Sam talk her into inviting Mason here in the first place.

Not that Mason would likely return, she decided, as she dropped off Sam at camp half an hour later. Trying not to scan the parking lot for the black Jeep, she felt disappointed nonetheless when she didn't see it.

By the time she pulled into the Griffin Davenport Riverwood Center parking lot, she remembered Mason had mentioned something about having an MRI on his knee this morning. The medical tests were the first step in returning to the life he loved, a life in which she and Sam had no part.

"Forget about him, Blair," she muttered, as she set about preparing Riverwood Center's interior landscaping for its grand opening next week.

But forgetting him was impossible, and she knew it. She'd spent half the night dreaming about him and the other half awake trying not to. It seemed as though all rational thought had been suspended and replaced with memories of the handsome, frustrating man from New England.

It was all for the best, she reminded herself. After their disastrous evening together, she knew she would probably never see Mason Walker again

With several hours to kill before picking up Sam from camp, Blair headed home. When she arrived, Mason's Jeep was waiting in the driveway. She eased her van past the dusty black vehicle, then scanned the front yard for some sign of him. Sam's dog followed her up the driveway, staying just far enough away to keep from getting caught under the wheels. Blair pulled around the house and into the narrow shed that served as a garage.

Slamming the vehicle into park, she cut the engine and jumped out. Instead of entering the house, she threw her purse inside the back door along with her keys and set out to find her unwanted guest.

Making a complete pass around the house, she finally gave up. Bubba followed her back into the front yard, suddenly interested in the strange vehicle. While the dog sniffed at the tires of the Jeep, Blair put her hand on the hood.

Still warm. He hadn't been here long, wherever he was.

She climbed the steps to the front porch and settled in the old wooden rocker to wait for him. He couldn't have gone far, she reasoned, then reluctantly patted the dog's head.

Bubba dropped down on the gray-painted boards and rolled over, inviting her to scratch his belly. She ignored him, her thoughts churning and the knot in her stomach growing with each passing minute.

For better or worse, Mason Walker was back in her life.

She'd wished for it and prayed against it many times during the long, sleepless hours of the night, but now that it had happened, she wasn't sure how she felt about it. Grandma Lettie always said to be careful of what you wish for because it just might come true.

For once, her grandmother had been right.

But had it been right not to tell him about her pregnancy? Maybe Mason would have welcomed the chance to be a father to Sam. "He's too busy playing games to be a father to that child," her grandmother had been fond of saying. "That boy's got better things to do than change diapers. He don't want you and that baby. He told me so when he called. And here you were in the hospital a-havin' that precious baby."

She hadn't doubted the truth of that statement then, although she'd wondered about it more than once over the years, especially after she committed her life—and the situation—to the Lord. No longer could she blame her choice to leave Mason Walker out of his son's life on her grandmother.

No, the decisions she'd made ten years ago were coming back to haunt her now. She watched a hummingbird flit around the bright orange flowers of the trumpet vine that snaked up one side of the porch while she tried to calm her fears.

Mason's intrusion into their lives was a sudden and, she hoped, short-lived episode. Soon he'd be back in Hawaii with his team, and she could get on with her life. He would never know her secret, and neither would Sam.

That decided, she craned her neck and looked down the road. No sign of him. Where could the man be?

Crossing her arms in front of her, she stopped rocking and leaned one foot on the post. In the distance, a mockingbird landed on the mailbox. Bubba gave a half-hearted yip, and it flew away.

A moment later, the mystery of Mason's whereabouts was solved when she saw him walking up the road toward her house.

six

Bubba raised his head, alert to the intruder, and Blair patted him in hopes of keeping him quiet.

Jingling his keys and apparently unaware of her presence, Mason headed for his vehicle, bounding across her lawn with a frown on his face and a cell phone in his hand.

Stuffing the phone into his shirt pocket, he opened the door to the Jeep and had one leg inside the vehicle when Blair finally spoke.

"You're in a hurry," she said evenly.

Mason's dark head jerked up in surprise at the sound of her voice. Shock gave way to a smile, and he turned and walked toward her.

Bubba leaped off the porch and met him halfway. He patted the dog on the head, but his gaze never left Blair.

"Hey. I didn't expect to see you here. Mind if we talk inside?"

"Why?"

Mason turned his back to her and picked up a rock Sam had left on the corner of the porch. In one fluid motion he sent it sailing over the fence and into the road. Bubba jumped to attention and ran after it.

"Because you and I need to talk about some things."

His voice shouldn't have given her pause, but it did. Nothing in his demeanor suggested he had anything of importance to talk to her about. She stood and gauged the distance between them. Too far and yet far too close.

෨

"All right," she said slowly. "I'll give you ten minutes to tell me why you're here."

She disappeared around the side of the house, and Mason heaved a sigh of relief. *What's she doing at home in the middle of the afternoon?*

"Okay, this is not a problem," he said under his breath.

All he had to do to cover his tracks was to come up with a convincing story as to why he'd driven all the way out here to take a walk. He could do that, he thought. After all, the best media experts in Major League Baseball had trained him. He knew how to say just enough without really saying anything. If he could deal with reporters, it would be a simple matter to work his charm on Blair without actually deceiving her.

He eased his worry down a notch. If Blair was home, Sam might be with her. That made getting caught almost worth it.

Then he stopped himself.

"Oh, boy," he whispered. "Is this what you're about now, Walker?"

He hung his head. *Father, I am so ashamed. What do I tell her?*

The front door opened. "You now have nine minutes to explain, and I suspect it will take every bit of that."

Blair's cool, soft voice shook him into action, and he followed her retreating figure inside. As his eyes adjusted to the interior of the house, he heard a curtain snap open, and his head followed the sound.

She stood in the window, her form silhouetted against the bright landscape of flowers and trees outside. Without a word, she sank down onto the window seat and pulled her legs underneath her, crossing them. The look on her face gave away nothing of what she might be thinking.

Mason took a deep breath, let it out slowly, and entered enemy territory with a smile on his face. What he was about to say, he had no idea, but he knew it had better be good. Stalling for time, he took a picture of Sam from the bookshelf. "Cute kid," he said.

"Eight minutes."

"Okay, I'll get to the point. I had an MRI on my knee this morning, and the doctors have cleared me to go back to the team after the break." He walked over to her and dropped into the nearest chair. "I didn't realize how much I missed hanging around with you until last night. I don't want it to end."

❧

His honesty stunned Blair. She found herself looking for something to say in response. Instead, she pushed a strand of hair off her forehead and contemplated the fringe on the brass lamp.

"You've raised a great kid," he said, breaking the silence between them.

Risking a glance in his direction, she felt an unwelcome jolt as their gazes met. "Yes, he is pretty great, isn't he?"

"And you did it alone. That's quite an accomplishment considering. . . ."

She lifted an eyebrow. "Considering?"

"Yes," he said. "Considering you lost your husband. Your second husband, that is. That must have been tough."

Warning bells sounded in her mind. She grabbed the nearest pillow, a floral chintz, and clutched it to her chest. How could he know this? Who had told him?

A car raced by on the narrow country lane, causing him to look out the window. "Care to talk about it?" he asked her.

"No. But you're down to six minutes."

His gaze swung back in her direction. A smile started on his face, growing in its intensity until she fully expected him to laugh aloud. "Fair enough," he said.

He leaned toward her, and Blair had the wildest urge to jump backward. Instead, she calmed herself by clutching the pillow tighter.

Then he touched her arm, and her concentration splintered. A jolt passed through her. She forced herself to ignore it.

"I'm waiting." She tried to sound stern but knew she failed when he smiled again and her heart started beating wildly.

"Okay. We had a good run, didn't we, Blair? I mean—what we had was something special."

"Yes, it was."

Her answer was a shade louder than a whisper, a reflection of her reluctance to answer. She clutched the pillow even tighter, fully expecting it to burst at any minute.

"And our divorce. We blew it by taking the easy way out, didn't we?"

There, the truth was out.

Blair met his gaze, and her shoulders slumped. "There was a time when I would have disagreed with you." She looked away.

"But now?"

Again she focused her attention on him. "But now I know better. As wrong as we were to rush into marriage, we were even more wrong to end it so quickly."

Mason was quiet for a moment. "I don't want to lose touch with you. I know that sounds strange, but not too many people out there can look at me and not see dollar signs." He pulled his hand away and studied it. "Let me get to know you again."

A tight knot formed in her stomach. She took a deep breath and began to count the tiles on the ceiling, exhaling slowly.

"Blair?"

She forced herself to speak, holding back tears. "Why?"

"Do I need a reason?" He paused and seemed to be considering his own question. "History. That's it. Even though it didn't work out between us, we have history." He leaned back in the chair. "Besides, that boy needs a man around."

❧

"Sam's doing just fine." She said the words too fast.

Mason knew he'd made a mistake. *Try again, Ace.* "Okay, you want the truth?"

She let out another long sigh. "That would be nice." He heard the dog bark twice, then fall silent. "And you have four minutes."

He took a deep breath and closed his eyes as he prayed for guidance. Then it came to him. *Just say it, get the truth out there and see what happens.*

"Okay, I just love being around him, you know? He's the kid I hope to have someday. I thought I could get in a little practice while I'm here. Find out what it's like to have a son of my own."

There. He'd said it. The truth, or at least a close approximation of it.

Ever since his first conversation with Michael Brighton, he'd been thinking how great it would be to have his son around on a permanent basis—to be a real father to Sam. Mason opened his eyes slightly and peeked at Blair, trying to gauge her reaction. Her fingers had gone white at the knuckles, and the frilly pillow she clutched to her chest was about to pop under the pressure.

She threw the pillow at him and stood abruptly. "I won't be an experiment in family life. Your time's up. Please leave."

Like the veteran infielder he was, he caught the pillow with one hand, dropping it swiftly to the floor with his other hand. And as Blair brushed past him to leave the room, he used his best defensive skills to stop her progress. "Wait."

ᕦ

Blair turned to face Mason. "Wait? That's the best you've got?"

For a moment, she thought he might say something, but all he did was shrug. And despite herself she felt a giggle rising.

It wasn't funny, really, the way he'd shown up out of the blue. But the goofy look on his face made her forget for a moment all that stood between them. He had come in peace, and she'd overreacted, listening to all those terrible things

Grandma Lettie had drilled into her brain, instead of giving him a chance.

Blair looked up at him. She couldn't think of the right word to describe him. She caught his attention and laughed again, and this time he joined her. The two of them laughing like kids brought back the best of times, days when the weight of the world had been far away and love had been all they needed to get by.

Blair touched the back of his hand lightly with the tip of her fingers. "Truce?" she heard him say.

"Truce."

She offered him something cold to drink, and he accepted. They walked back to the kitchen and sat at the old familiar table. Over iced tea and leftover pie, Mason began to regale her with tales of his struggle out of the minor leagues, his experiences along the way, and the extraordinary life baseball had given him.

Listening to him talk, a slight trace of his New England roots still evident in his voice, she felt a twinge of some foreign emotion. Jealousy perhaps? She couldn't be sure, but whatever it was, she knew she had no claim on it or him.

He told her about his place in Montana, and she watched his face soften. More years slipped away as he told her of the realization of another of his dreams, the purchase of several prize mares and a new stable of his own. She pictured him on the back of one of his cutting horses, man and animal working as a finely tuned pair, and knew he had all he needed in his life. This time when it came, she recognized the jealousy for what it was and pushed it away.

The fact that he led a full, happy life was as it should be. The fact that the life he led had nothing to do with her was her fault—and her choice—entirely.

By her actions, without his having a say in the matter, she'd given him the ability to lead the life he had. She'd spared him the heartache of giving up his dreams. But most of all neither of them had to watch what they had together slowly die as his resentment of her grew.

The reality of that thought soothed her as much as his close proximity had disconcerted her only moments before. Her aching conscience eased slightly.

Yes, just a couple of old friends spending some time together, she reasoned, as she watched the rise and fall of his chest from her too-close vantage point. *And Sam will be thrilled,* she decided, as she contemplated the fresh, masculine scent of his after-shave, the same fragrance he'd used when they were in love.

She could handle it if he could.

"I've been the one doing all the talking," she heard him say. The words jerked her back into reality with blinding speed. "Tell me about your life, Blair."

"M—my life?" Here it was, the moment of truth. She took a deep breath and let it out slowly. "Oh, I don't know. There's really not a lot to tell."

"Tell me anyway. Start with the day you left for England." His blue eyes, bright and clear, barely blinked. For a disturbing moment, it seemed as if that gaze were trying to peer into her very soul. "I want to know."

"Okay." She took a long drink of iced tea and set the glass back on the table. "I was so excited about the opportunity to study abroad, but when I got there, things were very different from how I'd imagined them."

He looked away. "Tell me about Sam's father."

What could she tell him? "It was all so sudden—and totally unexpected. I'd rather not talk about it."

The smooth, impassive expression on his face softened for a split second. "I see."

A drop of condensation slid down the glass. She watched it, unwilling to lift her gaze to face Mason. *Lord, please give me the right words. Don't let me hurt him any more than I have, but please don't let him find out about Sam.*

"Tell me about your son." His statement startled her.

"Sam's a gift from God, and I could never imagine life without him." That was definitely the truth.

"Any regrets?"

❧

A tear threatened to slide down her cheek. She wiped it away. "What I regret is that I had to lose you," she whispered. The power of that declaration slammed against her chest. She instantly wished she could capture those words and reel them back. Instead, she resumed her desperate dance on the edge of the truth. "Can we not talk about this anymore?"

He shifted positions, leaning slightly toward her, his elbows on the table and his hands cradling his head. "Do you know how long I've wanted to find out about you, Blair? I drove myself crazy for the love of you."

The look on his face told her he hadn't intended to say that. He closed his eyes, opening them slowly only to focus on something on the other side of the kitchen. He lowered his glass, releasing it when it touched the surface of the table.

Then the impact of his words hit home. He loved her?

But Grandma Lettie said. . . .

No, she couldn't consider the implications. He had to be lying. She felt the fragile truce begin to fall apart and scrambled to make things right again. "Hey, everything turned out okay, didn't it?" She forced a smile and reached across the distance to touch his hand. "You have had a great life."

"Yep." Finally, he smiled. "I guess you're right. And so have you."

"Yeah." *Oh, Mason, you have no idea.*

Pulling his fingers from beneath hers without warning, Mason stood and checked his watch, a gold and stainless-steel Rolex. *Another reminder of the differences in their lives,* she thought. She could pay off all her debts and put braces on Sam's teeth with the amount that timepiece had cost him.

"I'd better go help Trey before he tracks me down." He smiled. "I told him I'd be there by two."

"How is Trey these days?" she asked quickly.

"The same." Mason shrugged. "He retired three years ago, and now he sells mansions to movie stars out in L.A. He does these camps every summer to stay busy."

Blair smiled, thankful for the neutral subject.

They were almost to the door when Mason stopped and touched her lightly on the arm. "Let me bring Sam home after camp today."

She hesitated, trying to accustom herself to the idea. "Okay," she finally said. "If he doesn't mind."

"If he does, I'll call you. Where can I reach you?"

"I'll be home all afternoon. I have an armload of drawings to go over."

"Sounds like you're one busy lady," he said, removing his hand from her arm. "What is it you do?"

"Landscape design," she said. "Residential and commercial. I do office buildings mostly and a couple of restaurants and some private homes."

"For the guy on the phone?"

Was that a frown she saw appear and instantly disappear? She forced back a smile. "Yes, him and others. I plant the plants that everyone ignores, then keep them growing afterward."

He touched a dirt smudge on the hem of her shirt. "That explains this."

"I guess you could say I'm the supervisor and the crew. My business is still in the growing stages." She grinned despite her nervousness. "Pardon the pun."

Mason grinned. "But you're doing what you always wanted to do," he said slowly. "I'm proud of you for making that dream come true."

•

But how many much more important dreams had died? *Yes* was all she could manage. Then a thought occurred to her. "You never did say why you were here."

She thought she detected a stiffening of his shoulders. His face went blank, then he smiled and shook his head. "I came to talk, that's all."

He stepped out onto the porch and surveyed the front yard. Bubba appeared from out of the shadows of the oak, wagging his tail furiously. "Oh, about tonight."

Her traitorous heart leapt as Mason whirled around to face her. "Yes?" Oh, great—she sounded too interested. "What about it?"

There, that was better. Interested, but only in a casual, friendly sort of way.

"How about if I get Sam out of your hair and take him into town to a ball game? Trey and I have tickets to the college game, and we came up with an extra one for Sam if you'll let him go. We'll be out of your way all evening, and you can get lots of work done."

Her happiness plummeted. "Great."

"Something wrong?" Mason asked.

"No, nothing." She'd just been offered a rare afternoon and evening off without the responsibilities of parenthood. With Sam occupied, she would get a little extra time to work on projects that might someday launch her business into the realm of profitability. What could be wrong?

Mason nodded and turned toward the Jeep, then stopped a few feet away and patted Bubba on the head. Mason's blue gaze connected with Blair's over the distance separating them.

"Hey, Blair, thanks," he said. "For letting me spend time with Sam, I mean."

"Sure."

He drove away, and she watched him go through a fog of

swirling emotions. The man who'd arrived an enemy was leaving a friend, and she needed time to digest this. And fortunately, or unfortunately, time was something that was suddenly in great supply.

seven

Peanut shells, stray popcorn, and empty cotton-candy bags littered the stadium floor behind home plate where Mason, Sam, and Trey sat watching the game. After the ninth inning, when the last batter had been retired and the game ended, Mason stood and stretched.

"Okay, Buddy, let's get out of here."

Sam tugged on his sleeve and pointed to the field. "You said I could run the bases."

"I did?" His shoulders sagged. "Sure, Slugger." Mason tapped the bill of the boy's red hat and offered him a weak smile. "Go ahead. We'll watch from here."

Trey slapped his back and smiled at him. "Tired?"

"Nah, I'm fine."

Actually, nine innings with a nine year old had wiped him out, but in a good way. At this point, the job of Major-League second baseman looked easy compared to the job of being a dad.

"Hey, Mason!" a childish voice called. "Watch!"

On the other side of the fence, Sam stood poised to run the bases. Pride swelled in Mason's chest as the boy faked a home-run swing and took off in the direction of first base. The feeling grew into a full-blown ache as he rounded second. By the time he'd made it to third, Mason felt his eyes stinging. The twinge in his chest moved upward, lodging in his throat.

A big tear stung his eye as Sam slid into home feet first. Mason tried to hide the tear from Trey with the back of his hand, praying he could contain the rest before they fell.

74

"Something wrong?" Trey asked.

"Nope," Mason said, wiping the remainder of his emotions off his face. "Just something in my eye." He gripped the back of the seat in front of him, steadying himself.

"Oh. . ." Trey's voice trailed off as Sam trotted across the grass toward them. A look of recognition grew on Trey's face, and Mason felt dread course through him.

"Oh, Mase," Trey finally said. "Except for the color of his hair, he's the spitting image of you. He even has your swing."

"You're crazy," Mason heard himself say.

"Crazy like a fox," he answered, returning Sam's wave. "He's got your walk too." Trey pointed the empty cup in his hand toward Sam for emphasis. "I don't know why I didn't see it before. He's yours, isn't he?"

Briefly, he considered denying it, but he'd known Trey. "Yes," he said. "I'm pretty sure he is."

"Pretty sure, Mase? What does that mean?"

"Okay, he is mine, but Blair doesn't know I figured it out." Saying the words liberated something inside of him. At that moment, shouting his newfound parenthood from the rooftops seemed the next step. A step he'd dearly love to take if only he could.

"So what're you going to do about it?"

"Keep your voice down. I've got to go slow," he said. "I don't want her to run off again. I lost out on the first nine years of Sam's life, and I don't intend to miss any more of them." He gathered up the remains of Sam's souvenirs and started toward him with Trey following a step behind. "I'll find out the truth somehow."

"Buddy, the truth's staring you in the face." He pointed to Sam, who had made his way off the field and stood a few feet from them, absorbed in watching the grounds crew cover the field against the impending rain. "Won't be long before everyone else'll be seeing it too. Just look at him."

Before Mason could respond, Trey gave him a broad smile and disappeared into the crowd with a shout of good-bye. Mason grabbed Sam by the hand and went in search of the Jeep with Trey's words weighing heavily on his mind.

"So you've lived here all your life?" Mason asked casually as he pressed the power locks and cranked the ignition.

"Yep," Sam said, playing with the buttons that moved the Jeep's passenger seat.

Mason ignored the urge to tell him to stop. "Born in Tennessee?" he asked, watching the boy out of the corner of his eye.

"I guess." Sam tired of pressing that button and moved to another. "Hey, what does this do?"

The CD player screamed to attention, and a loud guitar solo filled the car. A second later, Mason snapped it off, and silence reigned again. Looking contrite, Sam settled back in his seat and pulled two pieces of candy out of his shirt pocket as Mason steered the Jeep onto the highway.

"Want one?" Sam flipped on the overhead light, temporarily blinding Mason.

"No, thanks," he answered, grasping the steering wheel firmly and focusing on the highway in front of them.

Sam unwrapped both candies and stuffed the sticky paper into the empty ashtray. "Watch this." He opened his mouth, revealing two round orange candies.

"Wow." Up ahead, a sign indicated the number of miles to their destination. Mason prayed for strength. "So the candy's round. That's great."

"No, dontcha see?" He opened his mouth again.

"Yeah, candy." *The boy was easily entertained,* he thought as he flipped off the interior light and turned onto the road leading north. "And it's round."

"No, look. It was red, and now it's orange. In a minute, it'll be yellow."

"Well, how about that?" Mason suppressed a smile. When had the ability to find joy in such simple things as color-changing candy and pushing buttons left him?

Thank You, Lord, for bringing me Sam. And thank You for returning my joy.

Concentrating hard on the candy in his mouth, Sam fell silent. Occasionally, he held it in his hand, checking the progression of colors through the spectrum of the rainbow in the light of the glove compartment. Each time he wiped his hands on something other than the paper napkin Mason had handed him, until finally the candy was gone and Sam fell asleep.

For the first time since he'd picked up the Jeep at Intercontinental Airport, he felt happy he wasn't driving his Porsche. Yet he was still glad the boy was with him.

His mind drifted back to Trey's claim that soon his paternity would become evident. He pondered the idea most of the way back to Magnolia.

By the time his tires crunched the familiar gravel of the driveway, he'd reached a decision. Lifting the boy's sleeping form out of the passenger seat, he carried him to the front door and knocked softly.

Opening the door, he stepped inside.

"Blair?" No answer.

He carried Sam upstairs and into the room at the front of the house where he'd seen him looking at the stars. It was easy to tell the room belonged to a young boy. Baseball posters lined the walls, and stacks of cards stood several inches high on the night stand.

As he settled the boy into bed, he saw that his current card lay on top of the stack. Near the baseball-shaped night light, a small picture of him in last year's Waves uniform hung on the wall. He smiled.

"Good night, Slugger." He removed Sam's cap and hung it on the bedpost, then headed downstairs to find Blair.

ᔝ

"Blair?"

Mason's voice floated toward her, gentle and soft. She smiled and tried to form an answer. Instead only his name escaped her lips.

Blinking heavily, she willed her eyes to focus. And when they did, she was immediately sorry. There stood Mason, both arms crossed in front of his chest, biceps straining against the sleeves of his shirt. On his face was a mischievous grin, marked on either side by deep dimples.

"Sorry, Blair," he said, taming the grin temporarily. "I didn't mean to wake you."

"Wake me?"

She looked around, a puzzled expression on her face. Finally, she realized she was sitting at her desk, a pile of slightly crumpled drawings under her outstretched arm, and the cloud began to lift.

"Was I dreaming?"

Another grin emerged, this one even bigger than the one before. "Yep," he finally said, his blue eyes twinkling. "And it must have been a good one because you said my name." He paused. "Twice."

"I did not!" She sat upright, trying to look dignified in her confusion.

"Afraid so," he said, chuckling. "Not that I blame you."

She tucked a wayward strand of hair behind her ear, refusing to let her embarrassment show. It was time to change the subject.

"Where's Sam?"

"He fell asleep halfway home," he said. "I put him to bed. His room's the one with the baseball posters, right?"

"Yes, thanks," she said softly, trying not to picture Mason's dark head leaning over her sleeping son as he tucked him in.

"It was my pleasure." Even through the fog of her sleepy

state, she could tell he meant it.

"Well, I guess I'll say good night then. I have an early start tomorrow. Eight o'clock meeting with my therapist."

She raised an eyebrow.

"Physical therapist," he said quickly.

"I knew that." They shared another smile as the clock struck eleven. "Thanks again for spending time with Sam tonight."

"No problem. Can we do something tomorrow, all three of us? Say six o'clock?"

"Tomorrow?" Fidgeting with a paper on her desk, she tried to swallow her anxiety and nodded. "Sure. What do you want to do?"

"Leave it to me," he said with a smile. "It's my turn to feed you two. Mind if I cook here?"

She mumbled something in agreement, and Mason walked over to the door. She watched him disappear around the corner and into the hall. A second later, he reappeared in the doorway, another mischievous grin on his face.

"Blair?"

"Yes?"

"You still snore."

Before she could deny the claim, he was gone.

❧

June 23

The morning, when it finally dawned, looked dreary, and by noon the gray sky had turned bleak with the possibility of more rain. Blair shoved away the thick stack of drawings and contemplated the pair of hummingbirds flitting outside her window. She stood to lose a small fortune in commissions because she couldn't concentrate, and it was all Mason Walker's fault.

"This is silly." She pulled the drawings back within reach

and removed the pencil from its place behind her ear.

Outside the sky threatened a much-needed shower, while inside Blair forced her mind back onto the work at hand. She unfurled the drawings and began to fill in the empty spaces with scale models of the plants she planned to use. Half an hour later, the blueprints of Griffin Davenport's private walled garden showed a space that would bloom with bright annuals and perennials, an elegant gazebo, and a lily pond situated in their midst. Satisfied with the results, she transferred the information onto her computer, rolled up the drawing, and began working on the next one.

A few errant raindrops spattered against the windowpane, their uneven cadence contrasting with the ticking of the old Regulator clock in the hall. Unbidden, Mason's face came to her again.

Rain.

It had been raining the first time they'd met. She closed her eyes and tried to picture him as he'd looked that day, but no distinct image would come to her, not as it did before.

Instead, she saw him as he was now, all the lines and imperfections that age had wrought, visible and endearing. The cocky kid he'd been on that first meeting had given way to the man he'd become, a man she had gradually begun to allow back into her heart despite her misgivings.

Thunder rumbled, and the wet pane answered with a small but audible shudder. She opened her eyes and watched the fat drops fill the deep ridges in the ground and clear the dust off the old wooden bench in the front yard.

Rain.

It had been raining the day Sam was born too. Through a fog of pain she'd called for Mason, knowing somewhere in her dulled mind he would never come. That night she held their child for the first time and listened to the rain. Every drop that fell mocked her, reminding her that Mason would be with her always, yet she would never be with him.

She could never bear to see the hatred in his eyes for saddling him with an unwanted child or even the betrayal on his face for not telling him. She still feared the same reaction. Ten years later, nothing had changed.

Except that he'd found her. Had God put them together again for a reason?

Without warning a bright shaft of sunlight cut across the page, bidding her to follow its path as it traveled over the scars and imperfections of the ancient wood floor toward the antique bookcase in the corner. Out of the shadows a wooden box painted with sprays of bluebonnets seemed to glow with the light that fell across it.

And she knew she had to open it.

Caressing the smooth wooden surface with one fingertip, she took a deep breath and let it out slowly. Another rumble of thunder sounded, this one distant and muted. Slowly she lifted the lid.

Tucked inside a circle of worn green fabric was a dirt-smudged baseball, her engagement present. A smile touched her lips. Warmth spread through her as she pulled the ball out of its nesting place and held it to her cheek. A thousand happy musings flooded her mind.

Joining the recollections of the past were the pictures of the present, images of Mason and Sam together. Suddenly, she couldn't be so sure about the decisions she'd made so long ago. They were adults now, mature people with lives of their own and a son that held them permanently connected.

Didn't he deserve to know?

But how would he react? Would he accept Sam as his son? She pondered this, thinking about what he'd told her about wanting a child of his own someday.

Someday, but not now.

Oh, Lord, show me what to do. I want to do Your will, not

mine, and I'm having a hard time with it. I have to think of what Your wishes are for Sam. Please give me some sign.

The phone rang, and when she picked it up she heard his voice. "Mason," she said, shoving the box back into the shadows. "I was just thinking about you. I'm glad you called."

Instantly, she cringed, wishing she hadn't said that. What was wrong with her? She sounded like a teenager, all tongue-tied and silly.

"You were?" She heard him chuckle. "Good or bad?"

"I refuse to answer that," she said, recovering her composure. "What's up?"

"It's about tonight."

Her heart fell. "Oh?"

"Yeah, something's come up."

"Oh." The sun hid behind a cloud, echoing her mood. "I understand."

"I'm expecting a conference call at five-thirty, so can we make it a little later, say at seven?."

The room remained cloaked in shadows, but her heart soared. "Sure. Seven it is. Is there anything I can do? Maybe dessert?"

There was a long pause. "Yeah, do you have any more of that pie?"

"You got it," she said softly, hoping that what she'd just heard had been some sort of convoluted male apology for his abrupt departure and hasty assumptions. "See you at seven."

"Hey, Blair?"

She touched the windowpane with one finger and traced the raindrop as it rolled downward. "Yes?"

"I'm glad you were thinking about me."

❧

As he hung up the phone and looked out the rain-splattered front window of the Jeep, he felt a little ashamed he hadn't told her he'd been thinking about her too. The sad fact was he hadn't been able to get her out of his mind ever since last night.

She had looked innocent and at peace in her slumber while he stood in the doorway and stared, unable to do anything else for a full minute, maybe two. When rational thoughts returned, he'd planned a quick escape, deciding to slip out the door without awakening her.

Then she said his name.

Her voice, hoarse with the effects of whatever she'd been dreaming about, wrenched a knot in his gut when he heard it. He'd moved closer. Then she said it again.

It irked him that he'd give anything to hear that sleepy voice calling his name just one more time. Surely he didn't really feel that way.

And by the time he reached his hotel room half an hour later, he'd almost convinced himself of that fact. Still, he took his time showering and shaving before looking in the closet for something to wear.

He wanted to give Blair the impression that the evening was no big deal, nothing for which he would dress up. Just another night out.

Discarding several other choices, he put on a pair of starched jeans and a white polo shirt with a Waves logo on the pocket. After consulting the bathroom mirror, he changed into a button-down shirt in a conservative blue-and-white pinstripe, then returned to check out the results, comb in hand.

While standing in front of the mirror, the big one in the dressing room with the fluorescent lights that showed no mercy, he had a startling revelation. The comb fell unnoticed onto the marble counter top as he moved an inch closer, turning his head to each side to confirm his suspicion.

He was going gray.

Strands of silver gleamed bright against his dark hair at each temple, their presence startling under the harsh light.

Immediately, he thought of pulling them out, but there were too many. Dying them was out of the question on such short notice.

He braved another look.

Maybe he had more than just a few, but surely no one would notice. Then he saw the wrinkles, a couple of fine lines that etched outward on either side of his eyes. Touching them with his index fingers, he stretched them until they were gone. Then he moved his fingers away, and they were back.

He remembered his agent's recent words, warning him of his advanced age. "Senior citizen," he'd called him, and for the first time in his life he felt old. He flexed his knee and wondered which part of his body would go next.

Self-pity was new to Mason and not a feeling he enjoyed, but he was alone in his hotel room and had plenty of time to nurture the feeling. "Snap out of it, Walker."

Falling into the chair beside the bed, he stared hard at the phone. He looked around the room and felt the walls closing in on him. Finally, he picked up the phone and dialed, knowing if he waited a moment longer he would lose his nerve and regain his powers of reason.

"Blair?"

"Mason?" The sound of that sweet voice saying his name did more than he cared to admit to ease his troubled soul. "What's wrong?"

"Wrong?" He ran a hand through the hair at his temple. "Nothing's wrong. I was just wondering. That is, if you don't mind. . . ." His voice trailed off as he tried to find the right words. Nothing casual or clever came to him, so he pressed on anyway. "My plans have changed. May I come over now?"

He found himself holding his breath and quickly let it out. The small silver clock on the dresser read a quarter to four.

"Now? Um, sure."

Relief and dread washed over him in equal parts, mixed

with something foreign. Was it anticipation? "Great," he said, stretching his legs to their full length and digging his toes into the plush white carpet.

"I need to pick up Sam from camp at five, but I'll be home after that." She paused. "Is everything all right?"

"Yeah, everything's fine. Everything's great," he said, trying to decipher his mixed feelings. He reached for his socks. "See ya."

"Okay."

"Oh, and, Blair?"

"Yes?"

"I've been thinking about you too." He hung up quickly, unable to believe he'd just said that and wishing he could take it back. Ten minutes later, he headed out the door, not caring that the owner of the Waves and the team's general manager were scheduled for a conference call at five-thirty to discuss his contract.

Let Morty deal with them, he thought. He gunned the engine and slipped into the freeway traffic heading north. That's what his agent was paid to do.

And what Mason got paid to do was play baseball. It had been too many years since anything but showing up at the ballpark had taken much of his time. Back home in Hawaii, he'd simply left his housekeeper a list of things he wanted, and they were there when he came home. Before that he'd been in college, dependent on dorm food, his grocery store outings limited to buying the weekend's ration of beverages and junk food.

Still, grocery shopping couldn't be that big of a deal.

He parked in the nearest place and hurried inside, determined to get in and out of the store quickly and efficiently. His watch read ten after four.

"Sure hope I don't get there before they do," he said as the electric doors of the Biggy Mart swung open and welcomed him inside.

eight

Nearly five-thirty. Where could Mason be?

The phone rang, and she ran to get it, hoping he hadn't changed his mind. When she heard Griffin Davenport's voice, she sank into the nearest chair with a frown.

The frown deepened when he questioned her about the projects he had assigned, the same items he'd asked about in an E-mail that morning. The man's presence over the phone felt as commanding as it did in person, and Blair wished desperately she had better news for him.

"I'm only looking at the general ideas. I don't expect a completed plan."

She scanned the thick column of blueprints lying rolled up on the top of her desk. What was wrong with her? Any other time she would have jumped at the opportunity to add another project to her list. She flicked an imaginary speck of dust off her best white T-shirt and studied the oak tree outside the window.

"Just fax me what you have."

"Right now?"

Blair thought she heard a chuckle on the other end of the line. "Yes, right now."

Panic surrendered to resignation as she discarded the possibility of pleading for extra time. If only she'd been able to concentrate this past week, she'd have something more substantial to send him. Just today she'd swept the porch, watered the ferns, lit the vanilla candle on the kitchen window, and performed countless other chores rather than work on the job at hand. Mindless tasks had commanded her attention, but one man had held it, refusing to allow her a single rational thought.

Now she had to face the consequences.

"Blair?"

Reluctantly, she answered him. "Yes. I'll fax the preliminaries right away. You'll have a formal proposal on each of the properties in two weeks."

Two weeks? What was she saying? She would have to shake off this cloud of confusion and work almost nonstop to meet that deadline. Thrusting her hand into the pocket of her freshly pressed khaki shorts, she gripped the phone and hoped he would tell her she could have as much time as she needed.

"Two weeks it is," he said.

Her shoulders slumped. So much for hoping.

Twenty minutes later, with Mason still nowhere in sight, Blair said a prayer for God's blessing and thanked Him for the possibility of more work. She started to press the send button on her fax machine, then stopped to glance over the documents one last time. If only Mr. Davenport had allowed her more time to do an in-depth analysis of each site before drawing up the preliminary designs.

In her business dealings, Blair prided herself on being professional and in control. *Her personal life was another story,* she thought as she saw the familiar black Jeep coming up the road.

A small fortune in commissions lay in the balance as she closed her eyes and pushed the red button. The machine went to work, the mechanical sound mingling with that of the car door slamming outside.

Turning her back on the fax transmission that could become the assignment of her life, Blair put on a genuine smile and went to meet Mason. When she found him, her smile grew into full-fledged laughter.

With plastic grocery bags dangling from both hands, he was struggling up the back steps with something large and apparently heavy wrapped in brown paper and cradled in the crook of his arm. He dropped the bundles onto the counter with a heavy thud and went back outside without a word.

"Need some help?" she called through the open door after he'd repeated this process several times.

The mountain of groceries he'd balanced on the counter began to shift. She lunged forward to right them, but not before two packages of carrots and a can of turkey gravy had fallen to the floor. She reached down and picked them up.

"Got it under control," she heard him say. A moment later, he came through the door again, his voice muffled by a package of sour cream and onion potato chips balanced on top of another assortment of bags.

A wayward lock of hair fell forward into his eyes, and part of his shirttail was hanging out of his jeans. He looked as if he'd just come back from battle—and lost.

"Where should I put these?"

Blair's eyes scanned the kitchen. Yellow and white bags covered every bit of available counter space, and the mysterious brown bundle now filled the porcelain sink. The table overflowed as well. Only the window sill, with the candle flickering, remained uncluttered.

She gestured toward the old Chambers stove. "Over there." She covered her grin with the back of her hand. "I hope that's the last of the bags."

Mason dropped three bags on the table and stepped back to admire his handiwork. A fat red tomato came rolling out, and he fielded it like a pro, tossing it back in one fluid motion. It landed on top of the brown bag and came to rest on the edge of the sink.

"Nothing left but the drinks," he said, glancing quickly around the room. "You get started on the turkey, and I'll clear off the stove as soon as I get the sodas. I'm starved."

"Turkey?"

"Yep." He fairly beamed with pride as he blew the dark lock out of his eyes with an upward breath. "It's my favorite. I bought all the things that go with it too." His face turned thoughtful, and his brows creased. "I hope you and Sam like turkey because if you don't—"

"No, turkey's fine."

She began digging through the bags in search of the ingredients for turkey sandwiches and found three different types of bread in the first bag alone. The phone rang, and she stopped to answer it.

Before she could continue her search, Sam burst through the door with a carton of orange juice in each hand and his baseball glove balanced atop his red cap.

"Hey, Mom, Brian invited me to go with him and his mom and dad to the Pizza Palace," he said as he wedged the cartons of juice between two grocery bags on the counter. "His dad knows the guy who bought it from the guy who used to own it, and he can get us all the tokens we want for free until it closes." Sam took a breath but only long enough to make a face Blair knew she couldn't refuse. "Please, can I go?"

"But Mason's here, and he's brought dinner. You really ought to stay home."

"Aw, Mom, Mason's cool and everything, but this is unlimited play in the game room. And we can stay till they close at ten 'cause Mr. McMinn says it's okay." He paused. "Please, Mom. I reeeaally want to go. If you let me, I'll never ask you for anything ever again."

"Yeah, right."

"C'mon, Mom. Mason'll understand." He paused, and she could almost hear the wheels turning. "Hey, maybe he could come too."

"No," she snapped. Instantly, she softened. "We'll have to talk about this. Mason was counting on your being here, Son."

And so was I.

The clock began to strike, and she realized it was only half past six, too many hours before ten. She opened her mouth to tell Sam she'd changed her mind about even considering it. Being alone with Mason Walker wasn't just wrong; it was dangerous.

"Cool! I know he won't mind. I gotta go put on my black shirt so nobody can see me in the virtual terrain hide-and-seek room."

The door slammed shut with a force that made her jump. "Sorry," she heard Mason say. "Didn't mean to do that. It's just that my hands were full and—"

She turned toward him, and he stopped talking midsentence, fixing his gaze on her, then dropped the plastic bags to the floor.

"What's wrong? Has something happened to Sam?"

Everything's wrong. I don't know how to be alone with you. Help me, Lord, to be strong. She realized she must have been frowning and quickly slipped into a smile.

"Nothing. Sam's fine." She took a deep breath and let it out slowly. "But he wants permission to go to the Pizza Palace with Brian."

"Oh?"

Was that the slightest hint of a smile?

"Yes. Something about unlimited virtual terrain. My next-door neighbor knows the new owner."

He ran a hand through his hair and looked interested. "Really? Cool."

"I didn't say he could go yet. Maybe you'd like to postpone dinner."

She tried to decipher the look that passed over his handsome face. Failing that, she leaned her back against the cool tile of the counter and feigned indifference, crossing her arms over her chest and gazing at the candle on the windowsill.

"Now why would I want to do that?" His voice flowed like honey. "I'm starving."

A yam rolled out of a bag and onto the floor, ruining her

casual pose. She picked it up and studied it, embarrassed yet grateful for the distraction.

"I mean, if you want to wait until Sam can join us, I'll understand," she said casually. "He did mention that you were invited to go along and play virtual whatchamacallit."

"You trying to get rid of me?"

She glanced up, caught him smiling, and looked down, clutching the yam as if it were made of pure gold.

Please, Lord, guide my words and actions.

"No. I just meant that if you felt uncomfortable about the situation—"

"Situation?" He moved a step closer, and butterflies invaded her stomach. "What situation?" Another step toward her, and she was sure he was close enough to hear the pounding of her heart, although he still stood a good distance away. "Do we have a situation here?"

Yes, we have a huge, confusing, wonderful situation here, she wanted to say. *A situation I've dreamed of and dreaded since the day you came back into my life.* Blair shrugged, rolling the thought back into the files of her mind where it belonged

She swallowed the truth and managed an answer. "No, but I thought—"

"Here's a thought. How about we eat first, then go check out the virtual whatchamacallit?" He looked around the crowded kitchen; then his gaze swung back to her. "How dangerous could that be?"

He punctuated the question with an innocent smile which broadened when, despite her best judgment, she agreed. The Walker dimples taunted her as he turned and began to dig through the bags stacked on the stove.

Finally, she looked away. *Lord, help me. I'm not the same woman he knew ten years ago, and I could never be her again even if I tried.*

Somehow the tomato in her hand slipped to the floor. Ignoring her confusion, Mason moved toward her with purposeful strides. Suddenly, the kitchen shrank.

"Here—let me help."

He brushed past her, leaving the spicy scent of after-shave in his wake. Goose flesh raised on her arms, and her heart did a flip-flop.

"No, really." Did her voice sound as squeaky to him as it did to her? "I can manage. Why don't you finish unloading the groceries?"

He shrugged and stepped back. "Okay."

She made sure she stayed out of his way as he passed, although the hint of spice drifted toward her.

"Where do you want these?" Mason asked, a half-dozen cans stacked in the crook of one arm. A loaf of bread and a package of dinner rolls teetered on top.

"Pantry," she said, exhaling sharply as she spoke the word.

She indicated the direction with her index finger, then began poking nervously at the mysterious item in her sink. Rock hard and cold to the touch, the thing appeared to be frozen. Surely this wasn't the turkey he expected her to prepare.

A thought occurred to her as she began unwrapping the bulky object. "Oh, Mason, be careful. There's a broom that keeps—"

"Ouch!" Cans crashed to the floor.

"—falling," she finished, whirling around.

Mason stood in the closet, one hand on his head and the other gripping a long yellow handle. He took a step back and lost his footing on a rolling can. Blair raced to catch him, dodging the broom as it shot out of Mason's hand and whizzed past her head.

Both of them landed in a heap on the floor, their arms and legs tangled and their noses only inches apart. The sound of breaking glass shattered the air as the broom connected with something fragile on the other side of the kitchen.

"Blair?" His eyes were closed; his breath blew warm against her chin.

"Yes?" The word emerged from her lips through a haze.

"Now we have a situation."

She thought she nodded. Numb, though, she wasn't sure until he smiled.

Warm, familiar lips kissed hers lightly. Their lips met again, a feather touch that tested their new and fragile friendship. Now, as with the last time he'd kissed her, all the old feelings came rolling back.

But this time it wasn't a kiss. It was an inferno.

And she could smell the smoke.

nine

Was that smoke he smelled? "Fire!" Mason flung Blair away from him and ran to the sink and what seemed to be the source of the fire. Sidestepping the still-rolling cans, he threw a dishtowel over the miniature bonfire, only to have the towel ignite as well. He reached for the faucet and turned on the water, dousing the flames and splashing soot-colored water everywhere.

Blair peered around his shoulder at the soggy mess.

"What happened?" She clutched his arm to steady herself.

He gave her a dazed look. "Sink. Turkey. Fire."

Their gazes met. Suddenly, she realized she was grasping his sleeve in her hand; she let go and backed away.

"I know," she sputtered. "But how did it start? It's the sink."

"I don't know." He stuck his hand in the murky water and pulled out a blob of grayish-brown wax covered with pieces of charred paper. "What's this?"

She took it from him, holding the object at arm's length. "It's my vanilla candle. The one I keep on the windowsill. But how—"

Her gaze fell on the broken windowpane, the empty windowsill, and finally on the mess in the sink. Several drops of water fell on her shorts, and she brushed them off.

"The broom must have knocked it off the sill and into the sink when you threw it." She handed him the dripping, shapeless blob. "You started the fire."

Sam appeared in the door. "Mason started a fire?" He peered at Mason, confused. "What didja wanna do that for?"

"I did not start a fire. And I didn't throw anything." He

94

leaned toward her until their eyes were level. "I was attacked. It was self-defense."

"Attacked?" She stifled a grin.

Just then they heard a car's horn honking, and Sam gestured toward the door. "Um, I don't have to help clean this up, do I? 'Cause that's probably Brian's dad."

Mason never looked away from her. "You go on, Sam," he said with a smile. "We'll take care of the mess and see you there in a few minutes. Save me a game, okay?"

With a whoop the whole neighborhood must have heard, Sam trotted toward the front door. "We won't be long," Blair called out before she heard the door shut.

Mason inched closer, and the room grew hot. Had the flames rekindled?

"I was attacked," he repeated. "By a broom."

Captured by his ice-blue gaze, she searched her mind for an answer. "Oh" was all she could manage, and that came out sounding more like a squeak than an actual word.

She pushed the dark lock off his face, unaware she was doing so, and saw for the first time the result of his bout with the broom. Her fingers lightly grazed the angry welt that crossed his forehead above his right temple. She felt him tense.

"You're hurt. I'll get you some ice."

"I'm fine, Blair." His voice was low and even.

Mason kept talking, but she couldn't make out the words. She leaned into the silken web of his whisper, allowing him to lull her into a calmness she didn't want to feel. Finally, his gaze returned to her eyes, and an awful, wonderful realization dawned on her.

She had slid sideways into the one feeling she had no right to have. Despite all she thought to be true about Mason Walker and all she could lose if she allowed the feeling to show, she knew without a doubt she had very nearly fallen deeply, hopelessly in love again.

A love she did not deserve.

She wrenched free and stepped away from him, knowing she couldn't risk allowing her emotions to take control. "I'll get that ice."

She'd reached the freezer door when his voice stopped her. "I never forgot you, Blair," he said. "You were always with me." He pointed to his chest with a sooty hand. "Here inside."

At least she thought it was his voice, though she couldn't be certain he'd actually said those words. She searched his face and still couldn't be sure. It was too perfect, the words too close to what she'd been hoping to hear.

Tell him.

Mason's hand reached for hers across the short distance, and she felt a pull that was more than physical. Their fingers touched, then hands clasped, as the last rays of the sun gave way to dark clouds. Outside the rain had begun again, a light summer shower that held the promise of becoming much more.

In the small kitchen, with the smell of smoke still heavy in the air, Blair felt something pass between them, a current much stronger than electricity, a bond that time and deception could never break. And she knew she had to obey the Lord's urging.

"Mason," she said softly. "Stop. This is wrong." He froze, then slowly released her. Wordless, his gaze captured hers. The smell of smoke tore at her eyes and wreaked havoc on her already delicate stomach. At least she tried to blame it on the smoke. "Let's go outside." She took his hand and led him out to the back porch.

She settled onto the old bench and fought the panic that threatened her. Taking a deep breath, she braved a glance at the man she was about to hurt, wishing with all her heart that things could be different.

Mason stood stiffly, hands stuffed into his front pockets, watching the drops of rain that fell from the eaves of the porch. Light spilled out from the open door and illuminated one side of his face, the other remaining cast in shadows. Dark splotches of soot streaked the front of his shirt, and the shirttail still hung out loosely, giving him the look of a little boy caught playing in his church clothes.

It broke her heart to see how much Sam resembled him. She memorized the moment, storing it away in case there were no more like it, then forced herself to meet his unwavering stare. "I owe you the truth about where I was the day we were supposed to meet outside Luigi's."

❧

"Before you say anything, I want you to know something." He dropped his gaze to study the toe of his boot. *Tell her,* he heard the familiar voice of his precious Lord whisper. Slowly, he turned his attention back to Blair.

"Nothing you say will ever make me stop—"

She looked puzzled, vulnerable, and confused. "Stop what?"

Loving you, he wanted to say. "Never mind" came out instead. Someday he would have the courage to say the words. Someday, but not now.

He just couldn't.

She glanced at him, and he felt an ache in his heart.

"Look—I'm not exactly prepared for this," she said. "I never thought we would have this discussion. Could you come and sit by me?"

His feet wouldn't move.

"Please." Her voice wavered. "It might be the last time you come near me."

Oh, great. He could see the tears in her eyes. If she had done him wrong, why did he feel like such a heel? Why didn't he put her out of her misery and tell her he knew about Sam?

Because he had to hear it from her, that's why. Because even though the old feelings had come edging back, a part of him hadn't forgiven her for what she'd done. For what she'd made him miss. And for judging him unworthy of the truth.

Above all, love each other deeply, because love covers over a multitude of sins. Forgive as I have forgiven. Release her to Me.

With those words echoing in his ears, Mason finally moved his feet in the same direction and took a spot next to her. Leaning forward, he rested his elbows on his knees and cradled his head in his hands, keeping her out of his line of sight.

He couldn't look at her. Not now. Not until he had his emotions under control.

She took a ragged breath, and he heard it, felt it, and tried to ignore it. "I don't know where to start," she whispered. "I've made so many mistakes. Which one do I admit to first?"

A big raindrop hit him on the side of the face. He ignored it, unable to muster the strength to wipe it away.

"I wanted to tell you, first before, then so many times after, but I didn't. I take full responsibility. I made that decision, and I was wrong. So very wrong. Long ago I asked God to forgive me, and now I need to ask you."

Release her to Me. Mason felt his spine stiffen.

"Mason, please look at me. I was on my way to Luigi's when I stepped out onto Prairie Avenue." She paused. "I was going to tell you about—well, my pregnancy wasn't something I could announce over the phone, and I wanted to make sure you really wanted—"

Again she paused, and another raindrop hit him square in the jaw. The wind blew others to join it. Still he couldn't wipe them away. His shirt collar dampened as he sat quietly and let her continue.

"I found out later that you wouldn't have been there anyway, but that doesn't matter. I still did you wrong, Mason, very wrong."

Tell her you were there waiting. Don't let her take all the blame.

He tried to speak but couldn't. All he could do was concentrate on the rain pelting his cheek and the drops rolling down his face and pooling on his collar. Then he realized it wasn't rain but tears that ran in streams down his cheeks.

She dipped her head. "Mason, Sam is your son. Our son," she amended. The words hung in the warm, damp air like the rain. Colorless, tasteless, odorless, but still very much there. "Mason, say something."

He tried but couldn't for the waves of peace and comfort washing over him, sweeping away all the anger and pain he'd accumulated over the past ten years.

Thank You, Lord.

She shifted beside him, leaning a bit away. When his gaze moved quickly to meet hers, she recoiled as if he'd hit her. "I'm sorry. I thought—"

"Blair, I was there, sitting on the bench outside Luigi's waiting for you. Then I called your grandmother. She told me you were in love with someone else."

Her gasp spoke volumes. "She told me the same thing about you," Blair whispered. "Oh, Mason, I'm so sorry."

The enormity of Lettie's deception rendered him mute. It did not, however, keep him from moving her closer into his arms until he found his voice.

"About Sam," he whispered. "I don't know what to say. God has blessed me with a—" His voice cracked and failed.

"With a son," Blair finished for him. "One you should have met long before now."

Wading in over his head, he could have happily drowned in her arms. The love he felt for Blair thrummed a chorus in his ears, still as strong as ever. Someday she would know how he felt. In the meantime, he knew he would never again hate the rain.

"We should go," Blair said slowly, her voice gentle. "Sam will be wondering what took so long."

Mason nodded, then looked down at his soot-stained shirt. "I don't think I can go like this."

"We're both a mess, aren't we?" Blair laughed and rubbed at the black smudge on her shorts, only making it worse. "At least the soot doesn't show on your dark jeans. I could probably find a T-shirt that would fit, if you don't mind wearing that."

He shook his head. "Thanks, but I think I'll take my chances on whatever I have in my bag in the car."

Blair smiled. "I keep forgetting you jocks don't go anywhere without your well-stocked gym bag."

She disappeared into the house and down the hall while he crossed the yard to the Jeep and pulled a clean shirt out of his bag. Slipping the soot-stained shirt off and buttoning up the fresh one, he wondered how he would spend a whole evening with her without telling her he was falling for her all over again.

Blair emerged a few minutes later in a pair of white slacks and a pink T-shirt that matched the blush on her cheeks. He knew right then that he was a goner.

"Ready?" she asked sweetly.

Mason gazed into her eyes and felt his heart lurch. "Yes," he whispered as he took her hand and led her toward the door.

❧

Blair basked in the warmth of Mason's smile as they strolled out to the car and headed for Magnolia's newest hot spot, the Pizza Palace. Of course, being a small town, the news of Mason Walker's appearance there had spread like a summer cold in sneezing season. The fact that her neighbor Marilee hadn't wasted any time telling anyone who would listen that the superstar had been seen next door probably contributed as well. This much was evident when they walked through the door.

And while Brian's dad, Harley McMinn, had been circumspect in his assessment of Mason, his wife Marilee watched him openly, even speculating on their relationship loudly on more than one occasion during dinner.

Still raw from the evening's confession, Blair sat in silence and listened to Mason's vague answers to Marilee's pointed questions. Beyond sharing the occasional small talk, she and Mason said little to each other; there had been no opportunity.

Before the night ended, Mason had signed autographs for everyone in the place, fended off more than a few bold females, and promised to get tickets to the next Waves game for the Pizza Palace's new owner. Handling the requests for autographs and free tickets seemed as though it came natural to Mason, but Blair sensed that ignoring the women may not have been as easy.

Time after time, whenever a woman approached, Mason would turn his attention to Sam or begin a discussion of some sort with Harley. As the evening wore on, he would occasionally lay his hand across Blair's or brush a lock of hair away from her face.

More than once she caught him watching her, only to smile rather than look away. Even when he seemed busy playing games with Sam, she noticed him looking at her across the restaurant crowd. In those moments, when their gazes met, the room seemed to shrink, and heat flooded her face.

Whatever the reason, whether out of self-defense or because he had a real interest in her and their son, Blair found herself basking in his attention with a happy heart.

This is what I missed, she thought more than once.

Later, after they'd endured the crowd and the virtual-reality games at the Pizza Palace, they returned to put Sam to bed together. While Mason lingered in Sam's room to read the next chapter of a bedtime book, Blair drifted out onto the front porch to try to make sense of the wonderfully confusing day she'd had.

Had she done the right thing by not telling him before? As

soon as the thought appeared, she pushed it away. Nothing would mar the happiness she'd found in the past three hours.

"Thank You, Lord," she whispered as she settled onto the rocker and lifted her gaze to the black night sky. "For bringing Mason back into my life."

"Yes, thank You, Lord," she heard a masculine voice say. She jumped to her feet to see Mason standing in the door. "For leading me back to Blair." He looked away, and when his gaze returned to her, his eyes seemed to be shining. "And for our Sam."

Covering her surprise and embarrassment, she offered him her hand as he opened the screen door and stepped outside. He sat down on a nearby chair, took her hand, and lifted her fingers to his lips.

"What're we going to do about this?" His voice sounded rough as sandpaper as he held her fingers against his cheek and smiled shyly at her.

Confused, she shook her head. "About what?"

The smile softened, and his gaze sought hers. "About us."

"Oh" became little more than a breath when Mason touched his finger to her lips and gave her a solemn look.

"It's difficult for me to be here," he said quietly. He looked away as if to collect his thoughts. "Blair, I'm a different man now. Changed."

She refused the urge to question him and pressed a hand to his, waiting silently for him to continue. What seemed like a lifetime later, he did.

"Baseball is important to me. It always was. But God has first place with me now. He's the head coach and general manager of my life. I'm just a base runner."

Her heart soared. "Oh, Mason, I'm so glad."

He nodded, almost impatient to continue. "I want to do this right, this thing between us. If there is anything, that is." He studied her fingers, then allowed his gaze to drift back to meet hers.

"We have to move slowly and wait for the Lord to guide us."

She smiled, slightly at first, then broader when she realized his meaning. He thought enough of her to wait and seek God's guidance on their relationship this time rather than rush into something that might be wrong. Something like their brief and disastrous marriage ten years ago.

"If only there were more time." He kissed her hand again. "In a few days I'll leave, and you and Sam will go back to the way you were before I came along."

"No," she said quickly. "No matter where you are, we will never be the same. Part of you will always be here." She drew in a breath. "In Sam," she added.

"I need more than that."

The words dangled in the air between them. "I understand," she said.

Mason leaned toward her, then abruptly swung back a step. "I have rehab in the morning, but I'll get to camp before lunch. I'd like it very much if you let me bring Sam home again."

"Sure," she said before she had time to think.

What if he said something to Sam? He wouldn't. Would he?

She opened her mouth to protest, and Mason covered it with a kiss. His hasty retreat seconds later left her reeling, almost as much as his parting words, spoken from the car.

"Let's not do that again," he said. "At least not until we decide on a more permanent relationship."

Blair raised her hand to her lips and, despite herself, blew him a kiss.

❧

Permanent arrangement? Had he really said that?

Mason rolled the idea around in his mind as he raced down the highway toward his hotel. Permanent arrangement, as in what? Suddenly, a picture of Blair sitting beside him on his porch in Montana, Sam astride his favorite cutting horse, came to him.

"Permanent arrangement as in marriage, that's what," he said aloud over the screaming guitar that blared from the speakers.

He snapped off the sound system, the loud music suddenly intrusive. When Mason reached his hotel, he tossed the keys to the valet. Ignoring the youth's curious stare, he entered the hotel lobby with the soot-stained shirt thrown over his shoulder and a smile on his face.

His expansive mood continued, even as he listened to the messages on his voice mail: three calls from his agent, one from Michael Brighton.

Strange—neither the Waves general manager nor the coach had bothered to leave a message. Pushing the save button, he stepped into the bathroom for a hot shower. When he walked out of the steamy room ten minutes later, he heard his cell phone ringing.

He picked it up, hoping it was Blair calling to tell him good night. "Miss me?" he asked and sank into the nearest chair.

"Well, actually I have," Lisa Rivers said.

Mason sat bolt upright, glancing at the clock. "Why are you calling me?" His rudeness should have made him ashamed. It didn't.

The woman laughed. "You're interested in information that might lead to custody of your son. Something damaging that would make the court see that his mother might not be the fit parent to raise him?"

He gripped the phone so hard the plastic receiver nearly snapped. "I never said anything of the sort."

"I'm sorry, Mason. I must have misunderstood."

He could almost hear the sugar dripping from her voice. It sickened him.

"Through some creative computing, which I will deny if put under oath, I was able to obtain a copy of his original birth certificate. Care to know what the boy's birth name was?"

"Look, Lisa—I don't expect you to understand this, but Blair and I won't need your services."

"Really?" Something in her voice put him on his guard once more. " 'Blair and I,' is it?" She paused. "Might I ask why you don't find me worthy of your valuable time? I mean just for future reference. Next time I get dumped, that is."

"You weren't dumped. There never was anything between us in the first place." Mason paused to send up a prayer for patience. "Look—how about joining a church singles' group? You'd meet a much better class of men."

"Maybe I don't want to meet a 'better class of men.' "

"Good-bye." Mason wearily ended the call.

&

"Oh, I don't think so, Mason."

Lisa pressed the switch to turn off her tape recorder and studied her perfectly manicured pink nails. An hour later, her carefully edited transcript was ready to be faxed. Happily she read her masterpiece, then slipped it into the machine and pressed the button.

ten

June 24

Blair had heard the humming start late last night and knew she had an incoming fax waiting on her desk. Instead of racing for the machine as she normally would, she strolled to the kitchen and refilled her coffee cup, taking it out onto the back porch. This morning Griffin Davenport, or whomever had sent the late-night fax, would have to wait.

Settling onto the little bench to sip her coffee, Blair allowed her mind to ramble across the events of last night. Her neighbor's greeting carried across the backyard. Adorned in loose denim shorts and a matching top, she wore a broad smile.

"Hi, Marilee. I didn't know you were outside."

"Honey, I don't think you even knew the sun was shining."

"What're you doing up so early?"

"It was either listen to Harley play video games with the boys or head for the yard. I picked the yard." She smiled. "Mind if I grab a cup of coffee?"

"Not at all," she said to her neighbor's retreating back.

"What happened in here?" she heard Marilee call from the kitchen.

"A little accident," she returned. "No big deal. Haven't had a chance to clean it up completely."

"Oh," Marilee replied, settling onto the wooden steps, coffee cup in hand. "So tell me about the cutie."

"Cutie?" Blair stifled a smile.

"Don't play dumb, Blair Montgomery. I saw the looks he gave you last night at the Pizza Palace. He's crazy about you."

"I have no idea what you're talking about." She paused to let the joke sink in. "And I'm kind of crazy about him too."

They shared a laugh, then lapsed into a companionable silence until Marilee finally spoke. "Seriously, he seems like a real nice guy."

"He is."

"Yeah, well, there aren't too many nice guys out there, so hang on to him."

"Who says there aren't many nice guys out there?" a deep voice called from the driveway.

Blair stood and craned her neck, her stomach doing a flip-flop as she saw Trey Wright turning the corner. Dressed in gray shorts and white T-shirt, a red ball cap covering his over-long tawny hair, he looked every inch the baseball player. He hadn't changed a bit, a fact she hadn't noticed the day she saw him at the ballpark.

"Trey Wright! What are you doing here?"

He covered the distance between them in several long strides, giving Blair a bear hug that lifted her feet off the ground. "Hello, Sweetheart. It's been way too long."

She held tight to her coffee cup to keep it from spilling. "It has been, hasn't it?"

"How many more of these do you have hidden around here?" Marilee said.

"Marilee, this is an old friend of mine from college. Meet Trey Wright. Trey, this is my neighbor, Marilee McMinn."

"So, Trey," Blair asked, "what brings you here?"

"Mason Walker, of course."

At the mention of Mason, Blair felt her cheeks grow warm. "Really? What about him?"

"Well, he's been actin' as if he doesn't have the sense the good Lord gave a goose, so I decided to come on out here and take the situation in hand. Make sure he's doing' right by you."

Marilee giggled. "I don't think you have anything to worry

about then. She and your friend had a great time last night at the Pizza Palace. There was a room full of people, but Mason Walker had eyes only for Blair."

Blair winced, studying the grass stain on the toe of her tennis shoe as heat flooded into her cheeks with a vengeance. "Is that true?" she heard him ask.

"Anyone want coffee?"

She jumped to her feet and headed back into the kitchen. Unfortunately, they followed her. Both of them.

"What happened?" Trey said, eyeing the sooty mess, the cans that littered the floor, and the burned turkey still floating in brownish-gray water in the sink.

"Mason cooked dinner." Blair took another cup out of the pantry, filled it, and handed it to Trey. As she motioned for them to follow her to the table, she whispered, "Don't ask."

"Ask what?"

Mason stood in the kitchen door. He produced a bag of donuts from behind his back and tossed it to Trey.

"Oh, Honey, you cooked." Trey glanced over his shoulder at the mess in the sink, then swung his gaze back to Mason. "Again," he added, his eyes twinkling.

When Blair saw Mason look at her, she was sure the fire that had erupted last night still smoldered. She felt herself grow weak and mushy inside.

"Well, it sure is hot in here," Trey said, shattering the silence.

"Definitely," Marilee added, fanning herself.

Mason greeted Trey with a hard slap on the back, then smiled at Blair's neighbor. "My session's cancelled so I thought I'd come by and pick up Sam on my way in." He glanced sideways at Trey. "Looks like someone beat me to it."

Ignoring the neighbor, he headed directly for Blair and kissed her tenderly on the cheek. "Good morning," he whispered.

"Coffee?" Blair asked

"No, thanks." He slid into the chair on Blair's right and wrapped his arm around her. Resisting the urge to wipe the lopsided grin off Trey's face, he reached for a cream-filled donut.

"So, Mase." Trey leaned back in his chair. "I thought I'd track you down and see if you wanted to do a little fishing today. Buddy of mine from prep school's a developer, and he has a sweet little boat docked out at the lake."

"No, thanks, Trey," he said, taking Blair's hand in his own. "Blair and I have some business to attend to today."

"Oh!" Marilee swallowed the rest of the donut in one bite.

"Family business," he added.

Trey's gaze met his, and he knew his buddy had caught his message. While visiting with the Lord this morning, he'd come to the decision that the first order of business had to be telling Sam the truth. After that, he and Blair could begin life together without any secrets.

The former catcher pushed away from the table and stood, reaching for another donut. "Okay, well, I guess I'll be going then. You sure you don't want me to take the slugger fishing so the two of you can have some private time?"

"No," they said in unison.

&

"I knew it! Brian told you about Peter, didn't he?" Sam plopped down on the overstuffed sofa and kicked at a cushion with his foot, sending it flying. "I can't believe my best friend in the whole world ratted on me."

"Who's Peter?" Blair asked.

"The snake Brian told you about."

"Sam, this isn't about a snake," Mason said, leaning against the door frame, his arms crossed in front of him.

Sam's eyes widened as he realized he'd let out a secret. "Oh," he said softly, reaching for the pillow and replacing it on the sofa. "I was keeping him in a coffee can under the porch, but I guess I gotta let him go now, huh?"

Blair nodded. "I doubt if he's happy living in a coffee can, Sweetie." She sat next to him on the sofa and tamped down her desire to scold him for keeping a disgusting reptile at all.

Sam appeared to consider her suggestion for a moment. "Yeah, you're probably right."

"Good. Now there's something a lot more important I need to tell you." She wrapped an arm around him. "Something that's very difficult for me. It's about your father."

Sam looked at Mason as if to explain. "He died a long time ago."

Lord, please guide my words and help Sam understand.

"No, Sam, he's very much alive." The boy's blue eyes widened, and she felt the guilt of her omission falling directly on her.

Then his eyes narrowed. "Then why didja tell me he was dead?"

Blair squeezed his shoulder and felt terrible when he pulled away. "I thought it was the right thing to do, but I was wrong. It was a bad mistake, and I'm trying to make it right. Do you understand that?"

"No. You lied." His blond brows creased into a frown, vivid against the tanned skin of his face. "You told me never to lie." He looked at Mason. "Never."

Relying on another quick prayer, she summoned the courage to go on. "What I did was wrong, Sam, very wrong. And I'm so sorry for the hurt that lie has caused. I loved your father with all my heart." She glanced at Mason, saw his encouraging smile, and returned it with one of her own.

Sam gave her a look that nearly broke her heart. "Why?" He shook his head. "Didn't you think he would like me?"

"Oh, Sweetheart," she said, gathering him into her arms again. "It was nothing like that. I. . .uh. . .that is, he—"

"He would have loved you very much," Mason interjected. "And he understands why your mother had to do what she did."

Sam's blond head popped up, and he eyed Mason critically. "How would you know?"

"Because I know."

His soothing voice was closer, though Blair hadn't noticed Mason's movement across the room. His hand joined hers, spanning their son's small back. When her gaze met his, her tears gathered in earnest despite her best efforts.

Mason wrapped his free hand around her, and they formed a tight circle. His head inclined toward hers, his expression tender and his eyes radiating a deep warmth that gave Blair the courage to finish what she'd started.

"Sam, look at me." He did, and his eyes, so like his father's, were two deep pools of blue that gave away nothing of what he might be feeling. "Sweetie, Mason is your father. There never was anyone else. I should have told both of you long ago, but I was afraid." A tidal wave of tears broke loose. "I'm so sorry."

"Be quiet!" The boy shrugged out of their embrace and ran from the room.

"Sam!" Blair jumped to her feet and started after him, but Mason placed his hand on her shoulder and stopped her.

"Let me," he said.

All she could do was nod. After all, who better to speak to her terribly wronged son than his terribly wronged father? She sank back onto the sofa, curled her legs under her, and listened to the sound of Mason's footsteps echoing in the quiet house.

She lifted her gaze to the ceiling. *Oh, Lord, help them both to forgive me as You have.*

۸

With each footstep he took, Mason grew less and less sure of what he would say to his son. Words of wisdom failed him, turning him mute as he slipped his hand inside the partly opened door and stepped into the bedroom. *Lord, speak to me and through me.*

To his surprise, Sam sat calmly in the middle of his bed, a notebook open in his lap. As Mason moved closer, he saw the book was filled with pages and pages of baseball cards. A couple of loose cards lay on the multicolored rug beside the bed.

The boy knew he was there, that much was certain, but something kept him from looking up from whatever he was doing. It was pride, Mason guessed, an emotion that seemed to run deep in the veins of the Walker men.

He knocked on the door behind him. No response.

"May I come in?" He watched Sam remove a baseball card from the album and send it sailing.

He tried a different approach. "Need some help with that?"

The boy didn't look up. "Nope," he said.

Mason took that one word as a small victory until he realized what his son was doing. Sam sent another pair of cards flying in his direction. Mason caught one of them and glanced at it.

It was one of his. They were all his.

"Okay, Sam. I get the point."

He dropped the card on the dresser, watching it land next to a picture of a Little League team dressed in red and white. Finding Sam among the motley group of boys, he picked up the photo and pretended to study it.

"I guess you're pretty surprised about all this," he said, returning the picture to the dresser. "I know I was when I found out."

Sam made a big show of turning the pages, never looking up. *At least he'd stopped throwing cards.* Mason took that as another victory for his side. He decided to risk moving closer.

"After the surprise wore off, I was really mad." He sank onto the bed inches away from Sam. "In fact, I was furious with your mom for what she did."

That got his attention. The book slammed shut.

"Yeah?" His gaze met Mason's, then skittered away.

"Yeah." Slowly Mason reached for the album, lifting it out of Sam's lap to place it on the floor. "But then you know what happened?"

Sam pulled his knees up under his chin and wrapped his arms around his legs. He gazed at a Houston Astros baseball poster hanging on the opposite wall.

"What?" he asked grudgingly.

"Well, first off, I prayed and asked God to help me understand what had happened." He paused. "Do you ever pray and ask God to help you with the hard stuff?"

Sam nodded.

"That's good. I guess your mom taught you how to do that, didn't she?"

He nodded again.

Mason folded his hands in his lap and fought the urge to gather the little boy into his arms. "The next thing I did was think about the good part of all this, and that made everything different. I stopped being mad and started being glad."

"What good part?" Sam asked slowly.

"The part where I found out I had a great son." He reached out and patted Sam on the knee. "Now I know you came up with the short end of the deal. Having me for a dad, I mean, but—"

"It's not you, Mason," he said, never looking away from the poster. "It's Mom." Finally, he pried his attention away and focused on Mason. "She lied."

"Yes," he said. "She did." He chose his words carefully. "But I believe her when she said she did it for us, for you and me. She's like that."

"Yeah," Sam admitted. "I guess you're right." He frowned. "But she still lied."

"Yes, she did. But you know what?"

He stretched out to lean on his elbow beside the boy. Fully expecting Sam to shrink away from him, Mason was surprised when the boy uncurled his legs and settled a few inches away.

"What?"

"The two of us have to forgive just as God forgives." He paused to clear the lump from his throat. "We're a family now."

Sam tilted his head slightly. "We are?"

"Yep. And we have to stick together."

"We do?"

"Sure." Mason rolled onto his back and supported his head in his hands, copying his son's position. "I know there are a lot of things you don't understand right now."

He wriggled a millimeter closer. "Kinda."

"Someday I think you will."

"I guess."

For a long while they lay side by side lost in thought. Finally, Mason spoke. "I love your mom, y'know? Always have, I think." Silence. "Someday I'm going to marry her again if she'll have me."

Sam lifted his head, his eyes open wide. "You and my mom used to be married?"

"Yes, we were," Mason said, "before you were born. And one of these days, when you're older, I'll tell you more about it. But for now, since you're the man of the house, I thought I ought to ask you if it's okay first."

"Oh." A smile lit his face. "Sure." He inched a little closer to Mason. "But you know she's not too hot on baseball."

"Yeah, I know."

"And she says the TV is just a bunch of noise." He scrunched up his nose.

Mason elbowed him playfully in the ribs. "You trying to talk me out of it?"

"Nope." Sam returned his jab with one of his own. "Just thought you ought to know." He paused. "Dad."

"Thanks," he said through the emotions that threatened to overwhelm him. His heart swelling with love, he gathered the boy in his arms and held him tight. "I love you, Son."

"Me too."

Ruffling Sam's hair, he offered him a bittersweet smile. "Maybe we ought to tell your mom everything's all right."

"Yeah, in a minute." He wrapped his little arms around Mason and hugged him tightly. "I don't wanna move yet."

"Me either, Son."

❧

Blair couldn't sit still another minute so she tiptoed down the hall toward Sam's room. She had to know how things were going.

The door stood slightly ajar, just enough for her to see Mason lying on his back, his feet hanging a few inches over the end of the bed. Sam snuggled on his shoulder, his little arm extending halfway across his father's broad chest. Both of them were sound asleep, their heads inclined toward each other as if, even in their dreams, they were sharing some special secret.

And both of them were smiling.

She stood and stared, basking in the wonder of the miracle God had wrought. Then she heard a phone ringing and ran to answer it. When she arrived downstairs, she realized it was Mason's cell phone but answered anyway to keep it from waking them.

"Yeah, gimmee Walker," the fast-talking voice said before she could utter a greeting.

"I'm sorry. Mr. Walker's unavailable right now. Could I take a message?"

She heard the man's rude laughter and disliked him immediately. "Yeah, I'll bet he's unavailable, but this is one call he'll want to take. Tell him it's Morty, and I have ten million reasons why he should answer the phone. Think you can remember all that, Little Lady?"

She opened her mouth to say something, then snapped it

shut. Instead, she slipped into her best Southern belle accent. "I'll sure try." She stuck out her tongue at the phone and tiptoed back upstairs to Sam's room.

"Mason," she whispered, tapping his shoulder gently.

He moaned and shrugged away her hand. Sam stretched and rolled onto his side, his eyes still sealed shut.

"Mason," she whispered into his ear. "Telephone. Some man named Morty."

His eyes slanted open, then closed again. "Tell him to go away."

"Believe me—I'd love to tell him that and more." She handed him the phone. "But he says it's important. Something about having ten million reasons for you to talk to him."

In one fluid motion, Mason was out of bed and down the hall. She thought she heard him laugh, but she couldn't be sure. Then the screen door slammed, and she knew he'd gone outside. She picked up the quilt from the end of the bed and covered Sam, closing the door as she left.

From the sound of things, whatever news he'd received must be good. He continued to talk, leaving her no choice but to find something else to do until he finished the call.

She remembered the fax she'd received this morning and went to find it. Griffin Davenport must have thought of more changes to the designs she'd sent him, something that happened on a regular basis these days.

Whatever the changes, she knew she could handle them. With Mason back in her life and the secret of Sam's paternity revealed, she was sure she could handle anything.

Blair stepped into the small office and reached for the document as another loud cheer erupted from the front porch. She smiled. Life was definitely good.

Then she read the fax.

It wasn't from Griffin Davenport.

eleven

Of course, Mason couldn't help but yell, even if he woke up the whole neighborhood. He was entitled. After all these years he'd finally reached his goal of earning ten million dollars—the magic number that told him he'd made it.

So what was the problem? He saw movement out of the corner of his eye and turned to follow it. Blair stood at her desk, a paper in her hand. She turned away, and he studied her back before she stepped away from the window and Mason lost sight of her. Instantly, he felt alone. He shifted positions, moving to another place on the porch where he could see her again. The dog followed, whimpering to be scratched.

Then he knew what the problem was.

If he couldn't stand to be out of her sight for more than a few minutes, how could he be away from her for the rest of the season? Three long months of pain and agony.

And his knee might give him trouble too.

"Mason? Hello?"

"Yeah, I'm here," he said as he pondered this latest complication.

"So do I tell the boys at the front office we have a done deal?"

He found himself hesitating. "I don't know. I have a couple of people I need to talk it over with," he heard himself say, surprised at how right the words sounded.

And, Lord, I'll be listening to You too.

"C'mon, Walker. Quit kidding around. I'm dying here."

Mason leaned against the wooden post on the porch and watched the love of his life reading the paper she held. "I've

117

never been more serious in my life, Morty."

He had a thought, a new and surprising turn of emotions that frightened him almost as much as it excited him. He realized he would gladly do anything she asked, even if it meant giving up the game he loved, to be with her. After all, baseball could hardly compare to Blair.

"Hey, Morty. What happens if I don't want to play in the All-Star game?"

Sputtering followed a long string of expletives that Mason barely heard. He was too busy watching Blair. And that bit of freckled shoulder glowing under the light of the lamp as she sank into a chair by the window.

"I'll call you," he said, ending the conversation with the touch of a button.

Leaving the phone on the porch rail, he went inside to tell Blair the good news, to warn her that she might be seeing more of him. When he stepped into the room, her pale, shocked face stopped him.

Without a word, Blair thrust a paper at him. He looked at her, her dark lashes spiked with tears, and felt fear slice through him.

"What's the matter?" He took two steps toward her before she backed away.

"Read it." She turned to face him, her eyes moist but bright with anger. "It's from your lawyer."

"My lawyer?"

The look she gave him sent a chill coursing through his veins. "Just read it. I found it very educational."

He scanned the document, unable to believe the words he read. The conversation he'd had the night before with Lisa Rivers had been edited creatively, giving the impression he had contacted her for the sole purpose of gaining custody of Sam. The conniving woman had even added a little note of her own for Blair, a warning that he was not the man he seemed and that it had taken a weekend trip to his cabin in Montana for her to find this out.

Dull anger bloomed into something more dangerous, more potent. He fought to regain control as the picture became clearer. Crushing the paper with one hand, he sent it sailing across the room; then he walked toward Blair. She cut him off with a sweeping gesture.

"It's true, isn't it?" she asked, her voice half an octave higher than usual. "It's all true."

He felt the rein on his emotions slipping and said a silent prayer for help. "Blair, surely you don't believe that garbage."

"Are you saying you didn't discuss my son with those lawyers?" Her look dared him to tell her anything but the truth.

"Our son," he reminded her, instantly regretting his choice of words. "And, no, I can't deny that I spoke to Mike Brighton about Sam. I'll admit at first I had some concerns—"

"Concerns?" She gestured toward the paper that lay on the floor near the window. "I hardly call trying to take my son away from me having concerns!"

"Do you really believe I'm capable of that?"

She retrieved the fax and held it in front of her, brandishing the white, crumpled paper as if it were a weapon. Finally, she opened it.

"Let's see what you're capable of, Mason." She consulted the paper again, and his heart sank. "Let's see," she said. "How did it go? Oh, yes, here it is."

She began to read, and his knees almost buckled. Refusing to give in to the feeling, he squared his shoulders and forced himself to remain standing.

" '. . .that might lead the boy to be placed in your custody. Something damaging that would make the court see that his mother might not be the fit parent to raise him.' " She looked him straight in the eye. "Tell me you didn't have this conversation."

Lying wasn't an option, and he knew it. "I can't, but I can tell you it didn't go down like that. Those were her words, not mine."

"Then she didn't visit you in Hamilton?"

"Yes," he said slowly, "she did, but I sent her away before she even reached the porch."

Blair's expression hardened, and her eyes glazed with what had to be unshed tears. At that moment, he felt lower than pond scum. The biggest idiot on the planet.

"Get out," she said in a voice that gave away nothing.

The words barely left her mouth, so soft was the sound. Yet, in the time it took for her to speak those two words, Mason felt his entire world collapse.

Wild with fear, he closed the distance between them and caught Blair up in his arms. "Don't do this," he said, searching for anything to erase the last five minutes from his life. "Please, Blair. Don't. I love you. Blair!"

But it wasn't Blair he held. Some stranger had taken her place. He could no longer reach her, and that terrified him.

She stood like a statue, her eyes a cold blue and her arms straight down by her side. "Get out," she repeated through clenched teeth.

"Sam," he said, pressing his hand against her back as if the gesture might return his Blair to him. "Think of Sam."

"That's exactly who I'm thinking of. And if you care anything about him you'll do as I ask and leave."

He stepped away from her and saw her push backward as if she were in slow motion. Somehow he moved across the room, distancing himself from her, and stood in the doorway.

"If I care anything about him?" *Get a grip. Try to understand what she must think of you. Try to see how bad this must look.* He grasped the door frame. "I was ready to give up—"

"Stop it! No more lies!"

She stepped toward him, her face a mask of conflicting

emotions: anger, hurt, and something else, something he couldn't name. Then she glared at him and turned away.

Disgust. That was what he saw there. That was the emotion he hadn't been able to name. And that hurt more than anything else.

"Sweetheart, look at me." She ignored him, her hands braced on the back of a chair. "I love you. I would never—"

She straightened her shoulders and tightened her grip on the chair. "Leave," she whispered, her plaintive voice tearing at his soul.

He stalled for time while he tried to think of what to do next. No way would he leave—not like this. He had to do something. "Let me call Mike. He'll tell you," he said, knowing he sounded like a teenager making excuses for missing curfew. He didn't care. He was desperate.

"Leave." This time the word was less of a plea and more of a command.

"But I love you. How can I leave you? Give me a chance to prove it." Now he was the one pleading. But he was past caring how he sounded. Beyond the slump of her shoulders, he gauged no discernible reaction. He knew he was about to lose her. "What about Sam?" he said softly. "What will you tell him?"

"I see no need to tell him anything beyond the fact that his father had to leave unexpectedly." She turned to face him, her eyes dry. "I think that's the best thing for all of us under the circumstances." She gave him a cold smile. "That is what you ballplayers do, isn't it? You do what's good for the team."

He could think of nothing to say.

"I won't keep you from Sam," she said. "Have your attorney call me, and we'll set up some sort of visitation schedule. But know this. You will not take Sam away from me."

"This isn't over, Blair," he heard himself say, the words reverberating in his brain until he thought the sound of them would never stop. He was back at his hotel, suitcase in hand, before he realized he could no longer hear them.

As he fastened his seat belt for the long night flight to Honolulu, he gave the matter to God and prayed He would tell him what to do. But as the taxi pulled up in front of his condo on Honolulu's Kalakaua Avenue, he couldn't help but add an additional prayer for God to hurry.

≥ **≥**

July 2

It was the kiss of a lifetime, one of those great lip locks you see in the movies, and Blair was in his arms. Then the phone rang, and the dream evaporated into reality. Mason lifted one eye, snapping it shut again when he saw the time. He found the phone and brought it to his ear.

"What?"

"Hi!" came the childish voice. "I got the box of stuff, and it's so cool. I'm wearin' the shirt, and this morning I ate your cereal, and I'd have the cleats on too, 'cept Mom won't let me wear them in the house 'cause they scratch the floor."

"Hey, there, Buddy," he said. "Gimme a minute to catch up with you." He shook the cobwebs out of his mind and tried to pry open his eyes.

As the room came into focus, his gaze fell on the clock again. He'd have to figure out a way to explain to the boy the time difference between Tennessee and Hawaii. He rolled over, escaping the shaft of sunlight that threatened on the horizon.

"After I talk to you, I'm gonna show Brian and Uncle Trey. He says I look like you so he's gonna be surprised when I really do look like you. You think my hair's always gonna be this color? It's okay, but I want it to be black like yours, only not with that silver stuff on the side, even if Brian's mom thinks it makes you look 'stinguished."

"That's distinguished." Mason shook his head and struggled to keep pace with Sam's rambling one-sided conversation. "Uncle Trey?"

"Yeah, he took me fishing last week. Anyway, I saw a lady on TV that changed her hair, and I asked Mom if I could do that, and she made this face and—"

He paused at his son's mention of Blair. "Hey, Buddy, how is your mom?"

"I dunno," he said, and Mason was struck by the boy's thoughtful tone. "She misses you a whole bunch."

He sat bolt upright. "Why do you think that?"

As he waited, his mind conjured up all sorts of explanations. She'd cried, of course. She'd probably broken down every time she saw a picture of him or heard his name on the news. He saw it all: Blair distraught at the grocery store, crying over the sports page. Blair in tears at the gas station when she heard a couple of guys discussing baseball at the next pump. Blair—

"Didja hear what I said?"

He pulled himself away from the pleasant thoughts. "No, sorry, Pal. What was that?"

"I was telling you my mom must miss you 'cause she never says anything about you, and she didn't even watch the Home Run Derby last night even though I told her you were gonna win it. And it was so cool you won. What kind of prize did you get? Was it a big trophy or a lot of money or a car? You probably won a car. Was it a Corvette or a Ferrari or something? Or was it—"

"Slow down, Sam. You're losing me here. Now tell me again about your mom. She misses me because. . ."

He heard Sam take a deep breath and exhale slowly. "Because she never says anything about you, and that's a dead giveaway."

"It is?"

"Yeah, dontcha see? When my turtle was lost I missed it a

whole bunch, and whenever I saw another turtle I got real sad so I stopped looking at turtles."

"And?"

"And I found my turtle again, and then I was happy again. It didn't bother me to look at turtles anymore."

This, Mason knew, made perfect sense to a nine-year-old boy. He, however, was more confused than ever. "So what's your suggestion, Pal?"

After a long pause, Sam spoke. "Okay, first you gotta get found. Y'know, like let it be a surprise. I was real surprised when I found Skippy, and that made it even better."

"Skippy?"

"The turtle. Anyway, if you sort of pop up like Skippy, then she'd be real glad, and she'd stop throwing the sports page into the trash and running into the bathroom when you come on TV."

Now that last part was interesting. "She throws the sports page in the trash and runs into the bathroom a lot, does she?"

"Only when she sees you. Yesterday I had to dig the paper out from under a whole pile of yucky tissues so I could put it in the cage with. . ."

His mind wandered, losing the last of Sam's sentence in the fog. Tissues? Another interesting fact.

"Yucky, huh?"

"Yeah, I think she has a cold. She's always blowing her nose, 'specially right after she sees you on TV. And sometimes I hear her blowing it at night when she's s'posed to be sleeping."

"Really?" So Blair was crying over him after all.

"I gotta go 'cause she's calling me."

"Okay, Son. I'm really glad you called. I'm here for you anytime you need me. Understand?"

"Yeah. I understand."

As tired as he was, Mason found himself reluctant to say

good-bye. He searched around for something to keep the boy on the line a little longer. "Hey, Son, you gonna watch me play today?"

"Are you kidding? 'Course I am. I wish I coulda come see you in person."

"Me too, Pal. Remember our signal?"

"Sure do," Sam answered. "You're gonna lift your glasses and wink, right?" In the background, his mother's voice came closer.

"That's right. You'd better go, Buddy."

"Okay," he said, his voice barely louder than a whisper. "I don't want Mom to know I've been talking to you. It might make her sad."

"Yeah." There were no words to tell his son how sad it made Mason. "Talk to you soon."

"Okay," he said. "Oh, and, Dad?"

At the sound of that word he felt a tightness in his chest. "Yeah?" He caught his breath.

"I love you."

"Oh, Sam, I love you too," he managed to say.

❧

Her heart would heal, she told herself. Blair tried not to listen to what sounded like a ball game going on in the next room. She threw a pencil at the sports page that lined the bottom of her trash can, without noticing whether she'd hit it.

Another rousing cheer went up from the other room. She tried to ignore it as she reached for the nearly empty box of tissues. Against her better judgment, she had allowed Sam to watch every possible minute of media hype leading up to the All-Star game being held this year in Honolulu.

And there had been plenty to watch.

Not being a baseball fan, she'd been shocked at the amount of time devoted to the sport over the past week. *It was indecent,* she decided, *the homage paid to a bunch of game-playing millionaires.* Not a one of them had found the cure for cancer, written a symphony or an unforgettable novel, or even contributed anything of value to justify their places in the world.

Bitter? She considered the idea, then discarded it. *Just the facts,* she thought. *That's all they were.* She picked up another tissue and blew her nose.

With the Lord's help she'd been dealing with this well over the past seven days, she thought, as she aimed the wadded-up tissue at the sports page. Of course, like everything else in her life lately, she just missed the mark.

"Mom, ya gotta see this," Sam called out to her. "Hurry!"

She closed the thick volume of building codes she'd been studying for Mr. Davenport's latest project, a huge renovation and landscape job at a Civil War-era estate called Honey Hill. Shoving her chair loudly across the linoleum in protest, she trudged into the living room to see what part of the monument to stupidity the TV cameras were focused on now.

And there he was in all his glory, the ultimate monument to stupidity—Mason Walker.

Tanned and handsome, he wore a dark-blue baseball cap backward, with a pair of sleek sunglasses cutting a black slash across his face. The shadow of a beard dusted his chin, and his ebony hair touched the neck of his blue Western League All-Stars jersey. A breeze lifted that one errant lock of hair forward, and he pushed it away with the back of his hand.

"Yeah, you know I never get tired of this," he was saying. "It was an honor to be out there playing with those guys today, and I thank God for giving me the privilege."

The camera zoomed in for a close-up. *Another few inches, and I can count his eyelashes,* she thought, looking at the traitorous man with disgust.

"I guess baseball's in my blood," he said. "My dad played the game, and I'm hoping someday my son will get a chance to do the same. Sam's already a decent ballplayer."

Sam squealed with delight. "Didja hear that? Didja? He said my name on TV."

"Oh, yes. I heard." How dare he suggest the boy might come close to turning out like him? Not while she was still drawing a breath. Not her child.

Then he lowered his glasses for a split second and winked at her.

Sam squealed in delight. "That's our signal," he said. "He did it like he told me he would."

"Signal?" Try as she might, she couldn't stop staring at the screen.

"Yeah, he told me he'd do it just for me. Look! He did it again! Didja see him?"

Oh, yes, she'd seen. Who was she kidding? She'd not only seen it; she'd felt it. One wink from him, and her nerve vanished.

"That's nice."

While the reporter asked him a question about kids and his being a role model, Blair turned to look at Sam. He was chewing happily on a mouthful of popcorn, his gaze fastened on the screen and on the man who would never be his role model as long as she lived. To her disgust, she noticed Sam was wearing a new dark-blue baseball jersey, one of those expensive items that must have come from his father.

On the back was the number one along with the name Walker emblazoned above it in bold letters. Just like the one his dad wore today on television.

Clenching her fists again, she took a deep breath, then exhaled sharply. "Sam, is that what was in the package you got this morning?"

"Yeah. Isn't it cool?"

"Way cool. It was a big box. Anything else in there?" So much for her decision not to pry. "Anything else interesting, that is?"

Sam gave her a funny look. "Uh, I guess not. 'Cept a couple

of gloves, a picture, a ball signed by all the Waves which was pretty cool, and the pair of cleats with real spikes on them that you told me I couldn't wear in the house. Oh, and a bunch of cereal boxes with his picture on 'em, and the letter he wrote."

"Letter?"

"Yeah, and he asked about you. Dad misses you, I think."

Dad. The word pierced her heart.

"Oh." She swallowed the lump in her throat, fighting the urge to jump for joy. She pictured him devastated, barely able to share his sadness with his son. "Did he tell you that?"

"Nope." He swung his gaze back to the TV screen and his father. "I just think it."

Joy crashed into disappointment. Blair turned her head to prevent her son from seeing her reaction. Unfortunately, her gaze landed back on the television and Mason.

The man looked straight into the camera and removed his dark glasses. His eyes, their blue irises seeming almost as large as a quarter, looked tired and bloodshot, and the lines around them were more pronounced.

"The knee's fine," he said in response to one of the numerous questions. "A little time off, and I feel like a new man."

A new man indeed. He looked like a man fresh from a party. Or a long night on the town.

❧

Mason sighed deeply and replaced the sunglasses over his tired eyes, trying in vain to listen to the post-game questions the reporters were throwing at him. One by one he answered them, using the trite phrases and meaningless words he'd been taught, giving them the sound bytes they needed for the evening news. They lauded his accomplishments, asking him how it felt to be playing ball again after his time away, and he answered, but not with the complete truth.

He would never tell them his time away from the game had been more painful than any injury and more wonderful than playing in any All-Star game. He would never tell them that, in the span of less than a week, his life had been completely and irrevocably changed, an experience second only to the day he let the Lord into his life.

The barrage of questions continued, the circle of people, cameras, and lights forming a tight barrier between him and the playing field he'd just left. He answered them politely and swiftly, not giving much thought to each, yet appearing to consider them before speaking.

"You've about done it all, Mason. You have a home-run record that will probably stand indefinitely, a fat contract on the table for next year, and almost every award a man can win in baseball. Is there anything you can't do?"

Mason jerked his head away from the cameras and lights, pushing away the senseless anger that overtook him as he sought out the face of the man who dared to ask him such a thing. It was just a question, another in the long line of stupid questions he'd been asked.

Why did the answer to that one cut him to the bone?

He replied with some flippant comment about not knowing what lay ahead and being thankful for the things he'd accomplished, or something to that effect. As soon as the words had left his mouth, he forgot them, to avoid thinking about the real answer.

Signaling the end of the interview with a sweep of his hand, he assumed a fake smile and sprinted toward the dugout, reminding himself not to limp. Finally, under the stinging hot spray of the shower, he allowed himself to consider the reporter's painful query.

"Is there anything you can't do?"

He heard the words echo in his mind and hated the answer that accompanied them. He couldn't do a lot of things, and most of them didn't make any difference to him. But the one that mattered, the one he'd give his life for, was to go back in time and change the events of the last ten years. He'd even settle for changing the past couple of weeks.

If he had the gift of time, he would have done things so differently. And he would still have Blair.

But time moved swiftly, and judgments were final. And that was the one thing all the home-run records and ten-million-dollar contracts in the world couldn't change.

He'd had his chance with Blair and blown it. Obviously, he'd misunderstood the Lord's leading on that one. Now it was time to go home and forget her.

And that's exactly what he'd planned to do, except that when he arrived at his hotel she'd left a message in his voice mail and stepped back in his heart as if she'd never left. "Mason," she said sweetly, "Sam wants to talk to you."

That was all. She gave the phone to the boy, and he rambled on about the game and how great it was that he remembered their signal and a few other things he'd hear when he replayed the message. For now he was too busy listening to that silken voice wrap itself around his name.

Without thinking he started dialing her number, then checked the time and almost hung up. He punched in another digit before slamming the receiver down. Seven long days without her and Sam, and it was all his fault.

He had to do something.

twelve

Time had never moved slowly for Blair. She stretched her neck, easing out the kinks with one hand and reaching for the manual of zoning restrictions with the other. It was the end of the first week without Mason, and she'd finally convinced herself that throwing him out had been the right thing to do.

Yesterday she hadn't been so sure, but today her resolve wasn't as weak. He'd called four times over the last seven days, eight hours and twenty-three minutes, and not once had he asked to speak to her.

Allowing Sam to call and congratulate him tonight had been the height of selflessness, she decided. After all, the man was his father. Besides, she thought, if Mason Walker wanted to speak to her, he could do so through their lawyers.

After all, he'd had no problem talking to lawyers before.

That decided, she blotted a big tear off the page she'd been studying, then threw the soggy tissue into the wastebasket on top of the others. She had her work, and she had Sam, and most important she had the Lord. She didn't need anyone or anything else.

Especially not Mason Walker.

She had plenty of ways to keep busy, she thought as she slammed the book shut and contemplated the ceiling. Stomping away from her desk, she headed for the kitchen to do something a little more mindless.

Half an hour later, she answered the phone on the second ring, her fingers dripping from dishwater and her nose stopped up from crying again. A huge knot stuck in her throat at the sound of Mason's voice. After a couple of false starts, she found her voice.

"Sam's asleep, Mason." She brushed her tears away with the dishtowel. "Did you want anything in particular? I could give him the message in the morning."

"Just wanted to talk. You know, thank him for the call." He paused. "I want to spend time with him, Blair," he said. "Can we work something out?"

"Like what?" she said with a gulp.

"We have a long home stand the first week in August. I want him here with me."

"He's too young to fly all that way alone."

"Then come with him," he said casually, taking her completely by surprise.

"I don't think so." She worked to keep her anger in check. After all he'd done, how dare he think she might be interested in flying to Hawaii for a visit? Why, he practically acted as if things were just fine between them.

"Be reasonable, Blair. I miss him and—"

"Reasonable?" Since when had she not been more than reasonable? "I was perfectly content to let you into our lives, and what did you do? You went behind my back and tried to take Sam away from me."

She heard him expel a long breath. "It didn't happen that way. The person who sent that doctored fax was fired and will most likely be disbarred. Besides that, she deliberately deceived you about what went on between us." He paused. "I care deeply for you and for Sam. Doesn't that make any difference?"

She gripped the phone so tight her fingers tingled. "You told me yourself that every word of it was true."

"The words were true, but they were taken out of context. When I realized Sam might be mine, I called a friend—"

"Who happened to be a lawyer."

"Fair enough," he said. "But I wasn't trying to take him away. Read the whole transcript of that conversation, and you'll see. After all that's come between us because of lies, why would I add to that?"

Why indeed? A niggling thought that he might be telling the truth teased her. "All right, Mason, I'd like to read that transcript."

"I'll see that it's sent." He paused, and for a second, she thought he might have hung up the phone. "Blair?"

"Yes?"

Another long pause. "Never mind."

The following morning a courier delivered a thick brown package bearing the return address of a law firm on Bishop Street in Honolulu, Hawaii. The top sheet was a letter, an official-looking document from an attorney named Michael Brighton. Beneath the letter was a file folder containing several more pages.

Scanning each page, she noted places where words seemed familiar. Just as Mason had said, the document in her hands was proof that the fax she received had been edited. In addition, it seemed painfully obvious that he and the lady lawyer had shared something more than an attorney-client relationship in the not-so-distant past.

Jealousy hit her hard even as logic told her she was crazy for caring. She bit her lip and exhaled slowly.

A pale green envelope slid out from beneath the pages and landed in her lap. Blair set the file aside and opened the envelope, taking care not to tear the delicate stationery inside. In neat script beneath the gold letter R were a single sentence and a signature.

"You win. Lisa."

Blair tossed the letter into the trash and dumped the contents of the file folder on top of it.

"You can have him, Honey," she said as she stalked away.

"I don't even want him anymore."

But as the words echoed in the empty room, she knew they were a lie.

☙

July 18

Mason leaned against the smooth black leather of the desk chair and laced his fingers behind his head. He watched the white-capped breakers pound the Waikiki Beach ten floors below and contemplated his dilemma.

Just looking at that fat file of legal papers made his stomach churn and his head hurt. To compound his troubles, Blair should have received all the proof she needed by now, but he still hadn't heard from her.

He shrugged his shoulders and let the rest of his concerns roll away. "I have ten million reasons for signing this contract with the Waves and only one reason not to," he said to his newly purchased pal, a gawky-looking Labrador retriever puppy named Jake, who lay curled at his feet. "Unfortunately, Blair's not speaking to me right now."

The black ball of fur rolled over and yawned, oblivious to his new owner's internal torment. Mason scooped up the little dog and settled him in his lap. He began to rub the scruff of fur between the puppy's ears, and in minutes, the little guy went limp with sleep.

On the desk in front of him, the contract lay open to the first page that required a signature. "Okay, Lord," he whispered. "It's Your call."

Then it hit him. With amazing clarity, the future lay before him, and he knew what the Lord wanted him to do with it.

After he counted the zeros on the contract twice to convince himself they were all there, he called his contract lawyer. He spoke briefly to Trey next, then phoned his agent to tell him of his decision.

With the reverence befitting such an auspicious occasion, he pulled the contract toward him and squared it on the desk. He picked up the expensive solid silver Mont Blanc pen Morty had given him after signing last year's contract extension and weighed it in his hand.

Jake began to whimper and wiggle, making little snuffing noises in his sleep. A deep sense of peace settled over Mason as he gave the contract one last, long look, then bowed his head to pray again. In his experience, it never hurt to check with the Lord before anything, especially something this important.

That night the Waves won a big victory over their opponent. The final score was due in part to the three home runs Mason hit in his four times at the plate, his best performance of the season.

Life was sweet, he thought to himself as he closed his eyes in the wee hours of the morning. And this time he didn't go to bed alone. Jake lay curled at his feet, soon joining his owner in a chorus of loud snoring.

Mason awakened to the puppy's tail beating a rhythm on his chest. "Today's the day the Lord and I start fixing this problem." He scratched the pup behind his ears, smiled, and reached for the phone.

"Hey," he said in his most cheerful voice when Blair answered. All of a sudden the line went dead. He hit redial. "Blair, we must have been cut off. Look—I just wanted to—" Again the call was disconnected, so he dialed the number a third time.

"Do not hang up," he said in his most commanding voice. To his surprise she complied. "Did you get the transcript?"

"Yes."

"And did you read it?"

"Yes."

"Well, what did you think?"

This time when she hung up he didn't call back. He did,

however, make a few more calls. In less than a half hour, his plan was set. Now all he had to do was wait for late September when the Waves played a series within driving distance of Magnolia.

"I can do that."

But as he said it he had little confidence it would be easy.

ᔤ

September 22

Sam pointed toward the jumbo jet approaching the terminal. "Is that Dad's plane?"

Blair sighed and nodded, wondering why she'd agreed to this meeting in the first place. She tugged at the neck of her sweater, then leaned against the broad expanse of glass separating her from the runway and tarmac.

She felt a yank on her sleeve. "He loves you, y'know." Sam twisted his face into a serious expression. "He told me so a long time ago. We're gonna be a family."

Knees weakened, Blair sank onto a bench and pulled Sam down beside her. Despite her feelings for the man, she'd been extra careful to keep Sam out of their problems, and she'd trusted Mason to do the same. If planting these false ideas in his head was part of Mason's game plan, she would nip it in the bud.

"Why would you think that, Sweetie?"

" 'Cause he told me." His attention returned to the jet now rolling to a stop outside the window. "I just don't know what's taking so long for him to do something about it."

"Maybe you misunderstood," she said slowly. "When did he tell you this?"

"The night I found out he was my dad. Way back in the summer." His gaze rolled back to her for a moment, and she saw Mason's eyes staring back from his innocent little face. "He said that he loved you and that we were gonna be a family, but it doesn't seem like we're a family. Why aren't we like a real family? I never even get to see my dad anymore."

Her heart sank.

What could she say? There were no words that could answer him without destroying the trust he had in his father, something she could never do, no matter what rotten, underhanded things Mason did. So she watched the man outside signal for the walkway to be attached to the plane and changed the subject.

"I bet you and your dad will have a wonderful time today," she said brightly. "It's really great he has a whole day and a half off before the big game tomorrow. You know that who-ever wins is going to the World Series."

She'd heard something about it on the sports channel last night. Not that she'd been looking for news of Mason. She'd just been flipping channels, and there he was.

He rolled his eyes. "It's way cool and stuff, but. . . ." His voice trailed off as he studied the luggage being unloaded from the plane.

"But?" She wrapped her arm around his little shoulder and gave him a squeeze, then let him wriggle free.

"But I wish you'd go with us. It's not that cold, and I know you don't like fishing, but I could bait the hook for you and take off the fish you catch, and you wouldn't have to touch anything slimy."

"Let's go down to baggage claim."

Blair gathered Sam in her arms and hugged him again before they walked the short distance. She tried to ignore the fact that he'd insisted on wearing the baseball shirt his father had sent him, despite the cooler weather.

A crowd had gathered at the baggage terminal. The time was near, and so was Mason. Her heart began to pound, and her head threatened to do the same.

Forgive him.

She shook off the words that had become too familiar over

the past two months. Sam pulled out of her embrace and smiled. "C'mon and go with us today. Maybe he'll ask ya then."

"Ask me what?" she said.

"To marry you, Silly," he said, giving her a playful nudge. "He already asked me if it was okay, and I said yes."

She stared at him in horror. What had the man been telling him? First he'd promised they would be a family and now this. Had he told Sam about the lady lawyer too?

His devious plan became crystal clear in her mind. He would be the good guy, the one trying to bring the three of them together, and she, by default, would become the bad guy. Well, she wouldn't let that happen.

Forgive him. This time the words rang louder than ever. She had to work extra hard to press them back into the corner of her mind.

Maybe she'd think about it tonight.

Forgive him as he and I have forgiven you.

Ouch.

Sam tugged at her elbow. "I figured he'd have done it by now, but maybe he's saving it for a surprise. Sort of like Skippy."

"Skippy? The turtle?"

"Yeah, know how it was such a great surprise when I got him back? Well, maybe that's what Dad's gonna do."

He climbed to his feet in the chair and tried to get a better look at the passengers coming toward them. Blair motioned for him to step down.

"Yes," she said, suppressing a smile. "It was a big surprise when you found Skippy."

How appropriate. He'd found the unfortunate turtle swimming in the toilet.

That image alone kept her sane and slightly amused for the last few minutes before the passengers emerged en masse through the gate. She'd get through this, she knew. Mason hadn't the least amount of hold on her anymore.

She was over him.

Yet the first dark head that appeared in the doorway set her heart fluttering. And it wasn't even Mason. She began to think about what Sam had said, trying to take her mind off the man who even now was making his way toward them from somewhere inside that plane.

He couldn't love her.

The idea was impossible to believe.

After all, it had been more than two months since their last lengthy conversation. Now she heard his voice more often on television than on the phone.

Not that she tried to watch or anything. Because most of the time it was an accident that she saw him. The Waves were winning, and he was about to break some silly record or something—that was all.

In the meantime, he'd spoken to Sam nearly every day.

Sometimes when she heard Sam and Mason talking, she felt a twinge. Was it regret?

Squaring her shoulders, she rose to her feet and pushed away the ridiculous thought. No way. She hadn't done anything to regret. If anyone should have any regrets it should be—

Mason Walker. Rational thoughts scattered when he stepped into the baggage claim area. He looked tired, she decided, as he met Sam halfway and lifted him into his arms. Across the distance their gazes met, and she rocked with the collision.

She couldn't force her limbs to move. Before she could regain her senses, he came toward her, a vision in faded jeans and black leather.

"Hi," he said casually, one arm holding their son, a battered brown leather satchel slung over the other. "It's been a long time."

"Hi," she heard herself say, although not as casually. "Yes, it has. It's been a long time, I mean. Since we've seen each other, that is."

How stupid did that sound? Where were all the witty comments she'd planned in the wee hours of the night when this creature's blue eyes kept her awake?

One look at him, and the grief she'd put herself through disappeared. Gone in the blink of two very blue eyes.

People moved around them, their bright colors and murmuring sounds swirling about as if this were a day like any other. But it wasn't. Mason had returned, and despite her best intentions, she was glad.

She shook her head. No, she couldn't be glad. Mason Walker was up to something. She could sense it. And whatever it was, he would not get away with it.

Still, he did look awfully handsome with his hair slightly mussed as if he'd been sleeping and his face tanned from the Hawaiian sun.

"You okay?" He regarded her with something like amusement.

Avoiding his direct gaze, she could only nod. What was wrong with her? This man tried to steal her child. How could she harbor any thoughts about him? She followed him through the airport and out into the parking garage, trying not to think of the answer to that question. And trying not to think. She did, however, manage a prayer for strength.

"Here it is, right where Trey said he would leave it." Mason stopped short in front of a little black sports car. "Just a sec, and I'll unlock it for you, Pal."

"Cool. Look, Mom—it's a Porsche," Sam said.

She mustered a smile. "Looks like someone bought a new toy."

If Mason heard her remark, he ignored it while he stowed his bag in the trunk.

"Wow, Dad!" Sam squealed as he sat down in the front seat and pushed the button on the door. "Where'd you get this cool car?" His seat began to rise, then lower. Then he pushed another button while Blair worked to stretch the seat belt across his middle.

"Sam, cut it out," she said, pushing his hand away and finally connecting the belt. "Sit still and mind your manners. I want you to behave while you're with your"—no, she couldn't say it, not out loud—"while you're with Mason."

"I will." He folded his hands in his lap, the model of good behavior. She saw the twinkle in his eye, however, and for a brief moment pitied Mason.

"Give me a kiss, Sweetie. I won't see you until tomorrow." She leaned toward Sam, and he cringed.

"Aw, Mom," he said before allowing her a quick peck on the cheek.

She stood and closed the door, whirling around to come face-to-face with Mason. Taking a step backward in surprise, she felt her foot slip off the curb. Mason caught her, and she landed with her head against his iron-hard shoulder and his arms around her back. The smell of leather mixed with a spicy scent permeated her senses.

With Mason's breath warm against her ear, Blair felt the ice melting somewhere deep inside her. Each rise and fall of his broad chest loosened its grip until only a lingering warmth remained.

It was like coming home. Only she knew this joy was not hers to claim. Obviously, Mason Walker was truly over her. She'd just have to get over him—again.

"Careful," he whispered against her neck. "You might fall and hurt yourself."

Too late, she thought as he released her and stepped away. Not that she'd ever tell him that.

"Are you all right?"

No. "Yes."

"It's good to see you again, Blair." Mason touched her sleeve. "I've missed both of you—a lot."

Their gazes collided, and Blair pulled away. The sincerity she saw in his eyes left her more than a little confused. How could he miss her unless—

Was the lady lawyer with the pale green stationery out of his life now? Had the best woman actually won?

She shook away the ridiculous thought and tried to concentrate on looking casual when she felt anything but that. "Sam's missed you too," she said as lightly as she could.

Mason grasped her fingers and gently pulled her toward him. "And what about you? Did you miss me?"

"Daaad! Come on!" Sam called.

"I'll have him back by noon." Mason backed away to open the car door and slid inside. "Game's at seven, and I have to get out to the field early. It takes a lot of tape and preparation to get me ready for a game nowadays."

She managed to nod. And as the car sped off, father and son riding with the top down through the crowded airport parking lot, she had to wonder if he'd felt anything when he held her.

thirteen

September 23

Blair awoke more exhausted than when she went to bed. Through the night God had dealt with her about her unforgiveness, and this morning she'd finally seen things His way.

The instant she released her pain to Him, the seesaw of her emotions settled down. How dare she hold a grudge against Mason when he'd so easily forgiven her of a much bigger hurt?

Blair smiled and leaned against the porch post. If God wanted the two of them to be more than friends, He would have to do the matchmaking.

As the sun rose over Magnolia, she promised Him she would take the first step to repair the relationship.

Just as soon as He showed her what that step was.

Finishing her coffee, she started working on the last of the plans for Honey Hill, the new project Mr. Davenport had contracted for her to landscape. Under most circumstances, renovating the grounds of the historic property would be an exciting proposition. With Mason Walker as a distraction, the excitement had lessened somewhat.

To that end, Blair placed a call to Hannah Andrews, the new owner of Honey Hill. After discussing everything from the weather to the next time she would bring Sam out to visit, she was able to finalize a list of specifications for finishing the greenhouse. Surprisingly, Mrs. Andrews had little in the way of suggestions for renovating the property. She'd left most of the decisions up to Blair, generally responding with a blithe "whatever you think best, Dear."

Barely a month stood between her crew and the projected completion deadline, and at the rate they were going, it would be close. There was so much work left to be done and so little time to waste. Still, she found herself looking up from her work every time she thought she heard a car coming up the road.

When the cloud of dust on the horizon finally produced a little black speck that could be the Porsche, her palms began to sweat. She rushed to the bedroom and took a few swipes at her unruly hair, finally giving up and capturing it in a gold barrette at the nape of her neck.

By the time the rumble of the powerful engine gave way to tires crunching on the driveway, she'd thrown off her old jeans and ratty T-shirt, exchanging them for a casual dress in a cheerful yellow sprinkled with white dots. As the car doors slammed shut, she slipped into her gold sandals and broke into a run, stopping a few steps short of the door.

Taking a deep breath, she wiped her sweaty palms on the back of her dress, then opened the door, feigning surprise.

"Well, hello, there, Sweetie," she said to Sam, ruffling his hair as he brushed past her with a package under his arm.

"Hi, Mom. Gotta go hook up this neat video game Dad got me. It's a. . ." His words trailed off when he disappeared upstairs and into his room.

And there stood Mason, too close and yet so far away, keys in hand. "I hope you don't mind." He handed her Sam's navy-blue Honolulu Waves backpack, and their fingers touched. "I bought him a little something. If you don't want him to have it, I can take it back. I'm sorry, but I didn't think to discuss it with you first."

"No, no, that's fine."

He said something else, but she missed it. Only a brain cell that hadn't been numbed by his presence alerted her to the fact. She shook her head and clasped the backpack a little tighter.

"What?" she said. "I'm sorry."

Please don't let him read my mind. Then he leaned forward, and she felt that magnetic pull again. This time she tried to fight it.

"I said I'd really like it if you and Sam would come to the game tonight. It's for all the marbles, and I'd like it a lot if you were there cheering for us."

"Cheering where?"

Think, Blair, she said to herself. What was it those beautifully chiseled lips were saying? The magnetic pull had begun to win.

"The game," he answered, giving her a look that told her he thought she was as crazy as a loon. "I brought a couple of tickets and arranged a car to pick you up in case you said yes." Then he smiled. "Please."

How many times had she heard him say that word in her dreams? "Yes" was her automatic response. It was a silly sort of whisper, and heat instantly flamed her cheeks. She cleared her throat and risked a look at him. "Sure, we'll go," she said, trying to act as if she hadn't just made a fool of herself.

He touched her hand, the one still gripping the screen door. "Great," he said. "I was afraid you would say no."

"Now why would I say that?"

Blair cringed inwardly. *Oh, wonderful,* she thought, she'd probably even batted her eyes too. What in the world was happening to her?

One minute he's a despicable creature, and the next minute he has me acting like Scarlett O'Hara to his Rhett Butler. This had nothing to do with the friendship she'd promised God she would pursue.

She pulled her hand away from under his, and the screen door almost hit her in the face. He stopped it in time with the toe of his boot, putting him in even closer proximity to her.

"Well, we did agree to deal with each other only through

our lawyers." He backed away, and she caught the door with one hand. "And I think that's probably the right thing to do. After this, I promise I won't bother you anymore."

She felt her hopes spiraling downward and bit her tongue to keep from saying the wrong thing. Slowly a prayer formed in her mind, and she sent it skyward. "You do?"

"No," he said slowly, "actually I don't." Leaning back against the porch rail, he crossed his arms over his chest and met her gaze with an intense look. "I mean, we owe it to Sam to spend a little family time together, don't you think?"

"Family time," she repeated, mindful of her promise to seek this man's friendship. "Yes, well, maybe so."

He nodded. "Definitely. I'm thinking once, maybe twice a week we'll schedule something with Sam—after the season's over, I mean. You know, dinner, fishing, a movie, whatever. Does that work for you?"

She could only echo his nod with one of her own. *Did he say fishing?*

"Good. I'm glad we got that straight." He punctuated the statement with a killer smile, then loped down the porch stairs and across the yard toward the expensive toy that passed for his mode of transportation. "Guess we'll be seeing a lot more of each other once I get moved into my place by the lake."

"The lake?" That was less than five minutes away.

"Yeah," he said, looking down at her over the top of his sunglasses. "Friend of mine's loaning me a place for the off season. Looks as if we'll be practically neighbors."

He slipped into the car and cranked the engine, then waved as he drove away. As she watched him go, Blair shook her head. The only thing harder than maintaining a friendship with her ex-husband would be reminding herself that a friendship was as far as their relationship could proceed, at least until the Lord told them otherwise.

The smile reappeared later that evening when he stood at

home plate and picked her and Sam out of the crowd. While he tipped his hat and winked at Sam, his gaze seemed to linger on Blair. Moments later, he hit his first home run of the night.

"Why are all those men beating on Mason?" she asked Sam over the din of the crowd.

"They're tellin' him he did a good job," Sam said.

"It looks like they're mad at him," she said, knowing that feeling too well. After all, he made loving him so complicated.

Loving him? Where had that come from?

She felt a hand on her shoulder and turned to see a woman of middle age smiling at her.

"I have a theory about that," the woman said. "I think it's because they all wish they'd done it instead of him."

"Makes sense to me," Blair said, sinking back into her seat to wait out the end of the interminably long game.

Every time Mason caught her looking at him, he smiled, and every time he smiled, she felt her stomach flip. When it was over, Mason's team had lost, but just barely.

And all she wanted to do was go home.

Settling into the comfortable limo for the ride back to Magnolia, Blair watched Sam brimming with excitement. His words were a constant stream that soon slowed to the occasional spurt. Before they reached the city limits of Magnolia, Sam had fallen into a deep sleep.

"Lord, what am I going to do about Mason Walker?" she whispered as she traced the curve of her sleeping son's chin.

Wait and be still.

⤞

October 12

As the Honey Hill project neared completion, Blair found she had less and less time to think about waiting, although she saw Mason more and more. At least she saw his car appear in the driveway, and she saw their son disappear into it as she headed off for another day at Honey Hill.

In the evenings, she returned home tired and less than sociable, wanting only a hot bath and a pillow. Sometimes Sam slept over at Mason's place, and other times Mason waited up for her until she arrived, letting Sam sleep in his own bed.

His entire social life seemed to revolve around Sam, giving a final rest to her worries about the lady lawyer. Tonight, as she peeked in on Sam to tell him good night, she caught Mason reading to him.

"Come in and listen, Mom," Sam called. "Dad's just getting to the good part."

She shook her head and took a step backward. "I don't want to intrude on a father-and-son moment."

Mason motioned for her to come in. "You wouldn't want to miss the good part, would you?"

Sinking onto the floor in the corner, she leaned her head against the wall and listened to Mason's deep voice wrap around the vivid prose of C. S. Lewis. Despite the tiredness that had permeated into her bones, Blair hung on every word until Mason stopped at the end of the chapter and turned to face her.

"This is the part where Sam and I say our prayers. Would you like to join us?"

Sam gave Mason an incredulous look. " 'Course she does, don't you, Mom?"

" 'Course I do," she said, imitating Sam as she climbed to her feet and crossed the room. Against her better judgment, she knelt beside Mason and placed her left hand in his. With her other hand she held tight to Sam. The little boy reached for his dad, completing the circle of prayer.

"You go first, Slugger," Mason said to Sam.

The little boy nodded, then cleared his throat. "Lord, thank You for that camping trip I get to go on soon and for fishing with Dad and his friends and for the nice lady with the big house at Mom's new job and for giving me my mom and my dad. . ."

Mason gave Blair's hand a quick squeeze. She cast a sideways glance to return his smile.

". . .and thank You, God, for letting them both be here tonight on account of how much I want them to be married again and live together forever and never get divorced again. Amen."

Blair's breath caught in her throat. Mason's fingers tightened around her hand. She refused to meet his gaze.

"Your turn, Mom."

"Heavenly Father," she said quietly, "thank You for this beautiful day and the star-filled night. Thank You for the blessings we've recognized and those we have failed to notice. Thank You for giving us Sam, and we ask that You hear his prayers and keep him safe through the night. Amen."

"Okay, Dad," Sam said. "Your turn."

"Father God, we come to You a family blessed beyond measure. We thank You for this day and ask that You keep us ever mindful of Your holy presence. Amen." Mason released Blair's hand. "Okay, Son, it's bedtime."

"Hey, no fair." Sam scrunched up his face into a scowl and folded his arms over his chest. "You forgot the part about Mom."

Mason cleared his throat and gave Blair a weak smile before turning to Sam. "Hey, that was supposed to be between us and God, remember?"

"Oh, yeah," Sam said.

Blair feigned irritation, her heart beating a furious rhythm and heat rising in her cheeks. "Are you two keeping secrets from me?"

"It's not a secret, 'zackly." Sam looked to his father for agreement. "It's kind of a—"

"It's getting late, Sam. Lights out, or your mom'll be mad

at me for keeping you up on a school night."

Mason had tucked Sam in and turned out the lights before Blair could get to her feet. She followed him downstairs to the front door and out onto the porch where she watched him pull his keys from his jeans pocket.

To her surprise he turned to face her. "Blair, you're working too hard."

She shrugged. "I love what I'm doing." The chill of the evening air felt wonderful against the heated skin of her face.

He studied her. "You really do, don't you?"

"Yes," she said, "I really do."

With a nod and a curt "good night," he set off across the yard.

"So what are you and Sam cooking up?" she called when she realized he intended to escape without making any further conversation.

"Wait and you'll see," he returned as he climbed into his car and sped off into the night.

"Wait," she whispered. Every time she took something regarding Mason to the Lord in prayer, she heard the Lord's words: *Wait and be still.* Now Mason was adding to it with a similar word of his own.

Exhaustion and the long list of last-minute details for Honey Hill's November eighth deadline waiting on her desk forced her back inside. When she had more time, she'd have to consider what the men in her life might be up to. For now, she'd just have to be still and wait.

❧

October 28

"How's the project?" Mr. Davenport asked, his distinctive twang drawing out the words. "Everything on schedule?"

Blair smiled. "Actually, it looks as if it'll be finished a day early. The painters are done, and all I'm waiting for now is the guys who put in the automatic watering system in the greenhouse. There's a problem with the timer. It goes on and off at all hours."

"But other than that it's all going according to plan?"

"Yes, it's going great. A couple of odd jobs left to be done, but nothing major. Why? Is there something wrong?" She heard the familiar sound of the Porsche pulling into the driveway and lifted the curtains to watch Sam and Mason unload their fishing gear. "You sound a little worried," she said, stepping away from the window to avoid being seen.

"Worried? No."

The screen door slammed, distracting her for a moment. Two voices, both talking at the same time, preceded the father and son into the room.

"You didn't either, Dad," Sam said. "My fish was the biggest."

"Wasn't either," Mason answered. "And we'll never know because they both got away."

"Didn't either. Mine got away, and you never did catch one."

"Did too," the deeper of the voices replied.

"Did not and dontcha even try to tell me something different."

"Company?" her client asked.

"What?" She watched them walk into the room. "Oh, no, it's just my son and"—she saw Mason's smile and melted inside—"and his dad."

"Well, then, I'll let you go," he said without missing a beat. "I'll see you out at the property in the morning."

She tried to listen, really she did, but Mason's presence made her forget the words as soon as she heard them. "The morning?" she asked, latching on to the only phrase that remained in her memory.

"The meeting is in the morning at Honey Hill," she heard him say. "Ten o'clock." He paused. "Is everything okay?"

Two matching smiles flashed in her direction as Mason

picked up his son and hefted him over his shoulder, carrying him out of the room without a backward glance. Sam burst into giggles, and the sound trailed him and his father as they left.

"Fine," she said, feeling the sudden chill of the empty room. "I'm fine. Tomorrow at ten. Honey Hill."

She could hear the sounds of a video game in progress, with both Mason and Sam carrying on a running dialogue punctuated by regular beeps and groans from the computer. Suddenly, the house seemed to shrink.

Escaping out the front door, she sank into the comfortable old rocker and took several deep cleansing breaths of the crisp fall air. Bubba eyed her suspiciously from his patch of sunshine near the mailbox but made no move to join her. She leaned her head back and closed her eyes.

With every creak of the rocker she thanked God for bringing Mason back to her only to beg Him to tell her why with the next conscious thought. Then she asked Him to tell her what to do next, to show her the way.

Wait and be still. I will make a way.

"I know, but don't You have anything new to report?" When further answers didn't arrive, she prayed for strength.

A couple of more deep breaths and she settled into an easy rhythm, rocking back and forth, with the only sounds around her the chirping of the birds and the occasional truck passing far off on the distant highway. Then she felt it, a subtle change in the air, a whisper on the breeze that only she could hear.

Her eyes opened. Mason Walker stood only inches away, a pained expression on his face. How he got there was a mystery she dared not contemplate.

"What's wrong?"

"Sorry. I didn't mean to bother you." He looked away, shrugging those broad shoulders. "I was about to leave, and I saw you just sitting out here and. . ."

"And?" She had the strangest notion that his eyes would

speak volumes if only he'd look at her.

"Forget it." Without a word, he turned and walked away.

"Lord, please let next week fly by," she whispered as Mason's Porsche disappeared from sight.

ঌ

October 29

Indeed, the next week did fly by as the big day drew nearer. Twice Blair saw Mason, but only from the front window when he brought Sam home. Her mind filled with a hundred details concerning her work, she tried not to think about him, something so much easier in the light of day.

But at night, when the day's activities slowed to nothing and the darkness closed in, she saw Mason often in her mind. Turning down the covers, she imagined his dark, wavy hair on his own pillow, as it would have been had their marriage continued all these years. Sliding between the white cotton sheets in the shadowy stillness, she felt him just beyond her reach, only inches away from her outstretched hand.

So close yet so far away. Until one night when she reached out and touched a living, breathing body.

"Mom," Sam's little voice said from the other side of the bed. "Can I sleep here tonight? I miss my dad tonight."

At that quiet, vulnerable moment with dreams of him still fresh on her mind, she had to bite her tongue to keep from telling Sam she missed him too. That's when she knew that the game she'd been playing, the one where she pretended she didn't love Mason, had gotten out of hand.

As she held her sleeping son, Blair finally heard the words she'd been waiting for. *It is time.*

Blair smiled and made a promise to God and herself that she would tell Mason how she felt, no matter what the consequences. And she would do it as soon as the Honey Hill project was finished.

The day before the projected date, Blair's work at Honey Hill was complete. She met one last time with Griffin Davenport and the architect, and their huge success put the three of them in a festive mood. Against her better judgment she agreed to meet them for a get-together after the final run through, one last celebration for a job well done. All that remained by Friday afternoon was a check of the outbuildings and then she could join them.

Clipboard in hand, Blair strolled toward the greenhouse, stopping short at the strange noise she heard. It sounded like snoring.

Striking out across the expanse of bright green grass that divided the newly tilled vegetable garden from the greenhouse, she opened the wood and glass door and peeked inside, searching for the offender. No one was around.

Instead, the tropical smell of warm, damp earth greeted her, a few of the hanging ferns still dripping from this morning's watering and the temperature still warm from the softly blowing heaters. She picked her way across the cobblestone floor to the back where the automatic controls were located. Checking the dials to make sure the settings were correct, she pushed the test button and watched while the newly installed automatic watering system burst into action.

Overhead, an assemblage of white painted pipes let loose with gentle streams of water, strategically placed to provide an even coverage for the large expanse of greenhouse interior. From where she stood, it looked to Blair as if someone had captured a rain cloud and set it free inside the room.

Satisfied, she reset the timer and left through the back door, emerging into the cool November afternoon, only to find the source of the loud snoring huddled against the greenhouse's large heating system.

She cleared her throat and waited for a response from the man who should have been painting the stables. Her only answer was a snort followed by a series of resounding snores.

"Mr. Collier," she said loudly.

Again nothing but snoring.

She kneeled down and touched his arm lightly. "Mr. Collier."

This time he opened one eye, regarding her critically from beneath the brim of his dark-blue baseball cap. "Yes?" he said slowly.

"Shouldn't you be doing something?"

"I was." His eye shut tight, indicating the conversation was over.

"Mr. Collier?" She counted to ten. Twice. "Mr. Collier!"

He adjusted his cap away from his eyes and glared at her. "What?"

"Are the stables finished?"

"Nope." He resumed his comfortable position. "Can't finish today. They're moving the horses in."

"Horses? No one told me horses would be moved in today."

She consulted the schedule attached to her clipboard. No animals of any kind were supposed to be delivered. Several pallets of Saint Augustine grass to patch the back lawn, four flats of Liriope to edge the cutting garden and ten yards of organic mulch for the vegetable garden were all expected this afternoon, but no horses.

"Does Mrs. Andrews know about this?"

"I reckon she does," he said, crossing his arms over his chest. "She's over there right now. Pretty animals they are. You oughta go see 'em."

"I will," she said, heading off in the direction of the stables.

As she rounded the corner, she stopped in her tracks and watched a large brown prancing horse being led into the unfinished stables. She sighed, shaking her head and making a note of her scheduling dilemma as she strode toward the barn.

A herd of horses was not what she needed to deal with right now. Especially not with the all-important deadline looming.

Steel gray hair blowing in the autumn breeze caught Blair's eye, and she knew she'd found Hannah Andrews. The older woman stood to one side, looking for the world like a general instructing the troops. Waving away a man in coveralls bearing a stack of papers, she headed toward Blair with a smile on her face.

"Still at work?" she asked with a smile. "I thought you'd be taking advantage of this beautiful day to spend time with your son. I so enjoyed his visit last weekend."

Blair frowned at the memory of Mason's sudden trip out of town last month, the one that forced her to bring Sam to work with her. Mrs. Andrews made an instant friend in Sam and had kept him entertained all day, much to Blair's relief.

"He's camping with the Scouts this weekend," Blair said. "And when he left he was still talking about the pineapple upside-down cake you let him help you make. I don't know if I thanked you properly for your hospitality. I hadn't intended to bring him, but there was a problem with—"

"Nonsense, Blair. I thoroughly enjoyed the boy." She smiled, her brown eyes twinkling in the bright fall sun. "I haven't had children around in years. It's a pity."

"Yes, they can be a joy, but there are the other times."

"That's true." Mrs. Andrews paused. "So I'll repeat the question. Why are you here when you could be with that darling boy and his father?"

Blair shook her head. "I'm trying my best to meet this schedule, but there's a problem."

"Problem?"

Blair nodded her head in the direction of the stables. "No horse deliveries were on the schedule for today. Is there anything else I should be aware of?"

Mrs. Andrews looked thoughtful. "Well, there is one thing."

She pulled her pencil out and prepared to write. "What's that?"

"Tea. You work entirely too hard." She linked her arm with Blair's. "Let's go have a cup of tea, and you can tell me all about your family."

"Family?"

"Yes," Mrs. Andrews said, practically dragging her toward a table already set for two under the gazebo. "I want to hear all about that adorable imp and his father."

"But the horses—"

"Don't worry about those horses," she said, pushing the back door open. "I've spoken to your Mr. Collier, and he's promised to stay late until the job is finished. I suspect he's gone off somewhere to catch a nap in case he's up late."

An hour later, the big iron gates closed behind Blair, and she drove down the country road with one last look back. "I sure am going to miss this place," she said under her breath as she slowed to a stop at the highway intersection, then headed to join her co-workers in an end-of-the-job celebration.

The Pines, a friendly, open-air restaurant just outside Magnolia, stood virtually empty late on that Friday afternoon. The only other patrons were a pair of leather-clad bikers drinking sodas and watching the news at the end of the bar. Blair paid for her mineral water and slipped into a green plastic patio chair across from Mr. Davenport and the architect, an energetic man by the name of Jack Delaney.

She listened politely as the men discussed various aspects of the real estate market. Soon she found her thoughts more on the decision she'd made a few nights ago than on profits and points. Tomorrow night was the big party, the house-warming at Honey Hill, and she'd decided to ask Mason to be her date.

It had been a big step, admitting he might be long-term commitment material after all, and while she'd accepted the fact in her mind, she wasn't sure she could actually admit it to him. She tried not to think of what he would say, of how he might react. The conversation around her turned to Honey Hill, and she forced herself to join in.

Speculation had run rampant over the party plans, which Mrs. Andrews had rendered top secret. Yesterday the house had been closed to all visitors, and even Blair and the architect hadn't been able to gain admittance. As she left this afternoon, the greenhouse had suffered the same fate, the beautifully leaded glass doors locked, the walls covered in white paper to disguise the goings-on inside.

For the life of her, Blair hadn't the foggiest idea from whom they were hiding the decorations, the location being about as private as any she could imagine. She chalked it up to the peculiarities of the wealthy.

She certainly hadn't learned anything by asking Hannah Andrews.

The mysterious crew of party planners, a varied group wearing badges and carrying clipboards, descended on Honey Hill with the efficiency of a SWAT team, closing the huge metal gates behind them and heading off in the direction of the house. Blair had lagged behind, her curiosity piqued, but she could see nothing of interest.

"I say it's going to be one amazing party," Jack said, raising his glass of iced tea. "Here's to the rich and famous. May they always be in need of a good architect. After all, I have three daughters, and they're marathon shoppers, right down to the five-year-old."

Blair felt Griffin Davenport studying her over his coffee, a faint smile on his perfectly tanned face. "Here, here," he said, his gaze unwavering. "Long live the new mistress of Honey Hill, and may her real-estate requirements be many."

She joined them in their toasts, saying nothing. Once again her mind had wandered elsewhere, caught somewhere between Mason Walker and abject loneliness. Then, in a cloud of dust and a squeal of tires, a car came to a screeching halt inches away from her van and brought her back to the present.

"Some people shouldn't have driver's licenses," she said to Jack who only nodded and smiled.

The car door slammed, but a large tree blocked her view of the driver. Footsteps crunched the gravel, and she knew the menace was about to walk through the door. When he did, she intended to give him a piece of her mind.

When Mason appeared at the entrance to the patio, her mouth went dry, and her brain went numb. Any words she'd intended to say were lost.

Once again she studied him, scuffed boots giving way to a long faded stretch of denim. Beneath the ever-present black leather jacket, he wore a white oxford shirt with a button-down collar that contrasted nicely with the mischievous look he wore on his face.

He'd driven with the top down; this much was obvious from the tangle of dark curls that flowed from the back of his base-ball cap. As he leaned against the wooden railing, his arms crossed over his chest.

Then he lifted a finger, moving it to his sunglasses in slow motion. When he pushed the black Ray-Bans on top of his cap, his blue gaze hit her like a pool of ice cold water on a hot afternoon.

She drank it all in, savoring the smile he gave her and offer-ing him one in return. At least she thought she smiled.

"I'll have whatever the lady's drinking," he said over his shoulder to the bartender.

"Mineral water it is," came the dry response.

"With lime." Mason's gaze slid back to meet hers. For a long moment, time stood still.

"Well, look who's here," Mr. Davenport said then, jumping to his feet to offer Mason a brisk handshake. "I didn't think you were going to show, Buddy."

fourteen

Mason shook his hand and said something to him, his gaze never leaving Blair's. Then Mr. Davenport introduced him to Jack Delaney, and he spoke again. Still the words did not reach her ears.

"Blair, I'd like you to meet a friend of mine," she heard Mr. Davenport say. "This is Mason Walker."

Mason took a few swaggering strides toward her until their fingers met, sending a shock wave to her brain that jolted her back into reality. She formed an intelligent answer in her mind that never quite materialized.

"Friend?" She stared at Griffin Davenport as if she were seeing him for the first time. Griffin was a businessman, and Mason was a ballplayer. How could the two of them travel in the same circles?

She looked to Mason for confirmation. "You know Mr. Davenport?"

He nodded, and the dimples deepened. "I get around," he said with a shrug.

With cat-like grace, Mason slid a straight-backed wooden chair up next to hers and turned it backward. He gave her the most innocent yet guilty look she'd ever seen, and her heart lurched again. It reminded her of Sam.

He sank down next to her. Because of the close space, his leg grazed hers. Every nerve in her jumped to attention, and she fought the urge to scoot away.

"Did Sam get that sleeping bag into the backpack I bought him?" Mason asked. She nodded and watched him sweep his vision away from her toward Mr. Davenport. "He had to carry all this stuff for the camp-out, and he was supposed to fit it all into his backpack so he could hike with it. I tried to tell him he didn't need the big one because it's so bulky, but the boy's stubborn." He nudged her with his leg. "I can't imagine who he gets it from."

"That's right," Mr. Davenport said. "He has the Scout thing. Left right after school, and he's coming back Sunday evening, right? That's all he could talk about at the lake last weekend. And that boy sure loves to talk." He paused and lifted his cup. "That and fish. He's better at it than you are, Walker. And I ought to know."

Before she could think of a reaction to that statement, the conversation veered in the direction of fishing and other things beyond her interest. She heard snatches of it, something about lake temperature and red wigglers, whatever those were, but she remained too surprised to follow it.

One clear truth began to emerge. Griffin Davenport and Mason Walker were on friendly terms—fishing buddy terms, of all things.

"Excuse me," she said evenly.

The male voices continued to swirl around her, paying no heed to her polite words. She tried again with no success.

"Hey!"

Her gaze locked with Mason's, and she automatically shifted into a friendlier disposition. "You've been taking my son fishing with the man who pays my salary, and I didn't know about it?"

He shrugged. "I guess." Mason resumed his debate with Griffin Davenport and the architect as if she hadn't said anything worth considering.

"But you accused me of—" She sputtered and worked to regain her train of thought. "You thought Mr. Davenport was my—" Heat flooded her cheeks when her client began to smile. "Never mind."

Mason leaned toward her and winked. "A good ballplayer always checks out the competition before he takes the field," he whispered.

Filled with the sudden urge to ponder his strange statement in solitude, she stood and touched Mason on the shoulder. Even under the leather jacket, she could feel his muscles jump on contact.

"I should be going. Could I speak to you outside?"

He lowered his drink to the table and gave her a slow smile. "Sure."

"See you tomorrow night," she said to the other men, making her exit as quickly as she could.

Tomorrow night.

Those words lay heavily on her mind as she reached the van, well aware that Mason followed a step behind. She fumbled with her keys, ultimately dropping them. As she leaned over to retrieve them, Mason's hand landed on hers.

His fingers enveloped her hand wrapping it in warmth. When he released her, she dropped the keys again. Fielding them with the expertise of a seasoned baseball veteran, he planted them firmly in her palm, then leaned against the car a few inches away from her. "Drive carefully" was all he said.

"Um, okay. Thanks." She looked away and filled her lungs with the crisp evening air. "How about dinner?" she asked as she exhaled.

Where those words had come from she had no idea. She braved a glance in his direction.

"Dinner?"

"Yes," she said, proud that it had come out sounding like a real word instead of the garbled mess she'd expected. She lifted her gaze to his and braved the impact, never wavering. "Dinner. Tonight."

"Can't." This time he looked away, and she had the distinct impression he felt uncomfortable with the question. "Plans.

You know how it is. Late notice and all."

"Sure. It's no big deal."

She wanted to die of embarrassment. Instead, she began to speak, something she regretted almost immediately.

"We all have to eat, and since Sam's away and I was going to anyway and so were you—I mean, I really didn't expect you to—" She affected a casual pose, nearly sliding sideways as she leaned against the freshly waxed surface of the van. "Oh, forget it."

Mason caught her by the arm, pulled her upright, and opened the door for her. She slipped inside and tried to fit the key into the ignition without looking at him. After two failed attempts, he reached over and did it for her.

"There's this thing." She paused. "It's for work. Anyway, I was wondering. . ."

She hoped he'd take the hint and jump right in with a resounding yes. Unfortunately, his handsome face went blank.

"You were wondering what?"

This was not going to be easy. "I was wondering if you'd—" She lost her nerve. "Never mind." If this was what guys went through every time they asked a girl for a date, it was a miracle the human race had survived this long.

"No," he said gently, laying a hand on her arm. "What thing? Do you need help with something for work? Is there anything I can do for you?"

"No."

She shook her head and averted her eyes, finally allowing her gaze to rest on the starched white collar of his shirt. "Never mind," she said, feeling the flush begin as she pulled out of his grasp and turned the ignition. "I changed my mind. No big deal."

But it was a big deal.

Without saying a word, he'd let her know that he no longer thought of her in a romantic way. Their brief time together seemed to be ancient history as far as this guy was concerned. He wouldn't even go to dinner with her, although he was quick to offer help for work.

What a pal.

Well, that was fine by her. She could go to the party alone. There was no shame in that. After all, she'd discovered long ago that no date at all was much better than a bad date.

Especially a bad date with a jock.

And given the uncertain status of their relationship, an evening with Mason might turn out to be a really bad date. She cast a furtive glance at the subject of her daydreams. *Or a really good one,* she thought.

In a flash, she left him standing in the parking lot, putting as much distance as she could between her embarrassment and the source of it. Half a mile from home the tears began. At the back porch, she decided she wouldn't give up that easily.

After all, the Lord had told her it was time to act.

"This is just going to take more time." She ran her hand over the wide porch railing. "But you will be mine, Mason Walker. Just you wait and see."

Blair arrived at Honey Hill the next evening wishing she were any place but at a party. What she really needed to be doing was working on her plans for recapturing Mason's attention, but business was business, and this was a command performance.

When Mrs. Andrews phoned that morning asking her to arrive promptly at six instead of the time of seven-thirty that was printed on the invitation, she'd found it strange. She forced herself to smile as she slipped into her shoes and grabbed her purse. At least she would get to see Honey Hill that much sooner.

But as she backed down the driveway, she felt less and less happy about her decision to attend the party. Even with Sam away on the camping trip, she thought staying home alone might be better than going. Twice she nearly turned back.

Postponing the inevitable, she passed the black iron gates twice before finally coming to a stop at the newly constructed guardhouse to surrender her engraved invitation.

"Drive on up to the house, Miss Montgomery," the guard said. "There'll be a man waiting to park your car."

"Thank you," she said, fighting the butterflies that rose out of nowhere in her stomach.

She drove slowly up the long, winding driveway past the horses that grazed in the pasture, the last rays of the sun disappearing into long purple, orange, and gold streaks behind the pines. Finally, the main house came into view, and Blair slowed to a crawl to admire the breathtaking sight.

Tall columns gleamed a brilliant white against the freshly painted exterior, the glossy foliage of a climbing rose framing either side of the double front doors. Twin chimneys flanked either side of the house, their presence in direct defiance of the architect Delaney's edict that they could never be restored to their former service. Looking at them now, the spires piercing the night sky, she was glad he'd been wrong.

Blair shook off the feeling of foreboding that had been troubling her since her arrival at Honey Hill and appraised the house with a more critical eye. Lights burned in every room, giving it the look of a brightly illuminated dollhouse perched on a carpet of green.

All around her the evidence of her hard work blossomed, literally. Layers and layers of green were punctuated here and there with bright splashes of color from the ancient camellia bushes, the only flowers in bloom this late in the season. She pictured the gardens as they would look in the spring, acre upon acre of flowers, both wild and cultivated, but all planted by design to complement the beautiful home they surrounded.

For one moment, she allowed herself to savor the pleasure of a job well done. Then a gentleman clad in a severe dark suit stepped out to meet her, ending her pleasant thoughts.

"Welcome to Honey Hill," he said, sweeping the door open with a formal bow. "You're expected, Miss Montgomery. Please follow me."

He led her up the front steps and into the large foyer, its polished marble floor reflecting the candles that shone from the original nineteenth-century chandelier above. She looked around and noticed for the first time that she was the only visitor in the house.

"Am I early?" she asked the retreating butler.

"Early, Miss? No, you're quite prompt." He continued his brisk pace down the hall and into the formal parlor. Still no other guests were in evidence.

His heels clicking an even cadence on the marble, he strode through the parlor and opened the large double doors that overlooked the pool and cutting garden, giving way to a thick cluster of yaupon and hollies.

"If you please, Miss Montgomery." He threw open the leaded glass door for her. "You're expected in the greenhouse."

"The greenhouse?"

The dour gentleman almost looked amused. "Shall I escort you?"

"No, I can find it." She stepped out into the cool evening air and pulled her grandmother's antique shawl tight around her shoulders. While the black dress she'd splurged on was long on style, it was short on warmth.

She had nearly lost her nerve and returned it. Twice. Then Mason Walker had turned her down, and she'd made the irrevocable decision to have a great time without him. Well, at least she could dress the part.

She cast a cautious look in that direction. "Are the rest of the guests out there?"

He only smiled and retreated into the house, leaving her with more questions than answers. And a very funny feeling that things were not as they seemed.

Black stiletto heels made for slow going across the paving stones that formed a path between the main house and the secluded greenhouse. Once the pool and patio had disappeared behind her, Blair slipped off the offending shoes and made her way down the twisting, turning path much faster.

At the door to the massive Victorian structure, she stopped, leaning against the freshly painted white wood trim, and slipped back into her shoes. Then she felt it. Someone was nearby.

"Well, of course, Silly," she said under her breath as she took a tentative step forward. "Mrs. Andrews is waiting for me in there."

But the greenhouse was too dimly lit to be occupied. Or at least it seemed that way from the outside.

She nearly turned back; then she heard the music, a soft soulful sound that seemed to be coming from inside. Putting her ear to the glass, she heard the rise and fall of a saxophone, a rhythm that almost matched the beating of her heart.

When she opened the door, the music swelled, and so did the lump in her throat. Far from being dark, the lush interior basked in the glow of a thousand ivory candles. From the rafters, strings of tiny white lights glittered like lightning bugs on a hot summer night.

Leaving the crisp night air outside, she pulled the door shut and turned to admire the sparkling room. Dark green foliage and a rainbow of hothouse flowers held court with a thousand pinpoints of light.

In the open center of the structure, a table covered in pale cream fabric had been set up with two glasses and a bottle of mineral water chilling in a silver bucket adorned with limes. A gift wrapped in creamy paper and tied with a large silver bow flanked the bucket, a bright profusion of blue and white flowers filling a cut crystal vase behind them.

On either side stood twin chaise lounges thickly padded with a profusion of multicolored chintz pillows. Across from them were two more, forming a tight conversation group that transformed the utilitarian greenhouse into a welcoming space.

One of Mrs. Andrews's more frivolous purchases, Blair had tried to warn her they wouldn't last six months in the warm and humid environment. Seeing them in the glow of the candles, she could understand the reason the woman had insisted on having them.

It was a lovely backdrop for a party, although she couldn't imagine more than twenty or thirty people could have been invited. Any more than that and the guests would be standing elbow to elbow. A movement along the back of the room caught her attention.

"Mrs. Andrews?"

No answer.

She stood still and tried to listen above the music and the pounding of her heart, the urge to run nearly overwhelming her.

"Who's there?" She took a cautious step backward, then another. "Look—it's obvious there's been a mistake. I'll be going now." On the third step backward, she slipped out of her heels. "I'll come back later when the rest of the guests are here."

"Don't go."

The voice filled the room, and her knees went weak. "Mason?"

He stepped into view wearing a black tuxedo and a smile. "Stay. Please?"

She cocked her head to one side and stared at him. "What are you doing here? You said you had plans."

He countered with a look so innocent she knew he had to be guilty of something. "I did. I planned to be here."

Footsteps rang out a warning that he was approaching although she lost him in the play of light and shadows. "Don't tell me you know Mrs. Andrews too."

"You might say that." Then he materialized beside her, blocking out the light and filling the space with his presence.

"Do you and Sam fish with her too?"

"No."

She waited for the smile that never appeared; somehow her shawl slipped to the ground, but she couldn't bring herself to look for it.

Soft music filled the silence as she tried to think of something to say. Mason seemed to move closer, inching toward her, although she knew he hadn't moved at all.

"Why am I here?" she finally managed to ask.

"To settle some things." He bridged the gap between them by clasping her hand.

"About Sam?"

"That's part of it."

"I see." She looked down at his fingers, weaving together with hers, and wondered how she'd ever managed to set him free.

"I was thinking—"

She stopped his words with a kiss.

An arm went around her waist, an unyielding steel band covered in velvet that took her breath away. He released her fingers only to capture her completely in the circle of his embrace. Lost in the moment, she almost didn't feel her feet leaving the ground.

"Your knee," she whispered against his lips. "Put me down. How're you going to earn that ten million dollars if you're hurt?"

"I'm not," he said, depositing her on the chaise. "Turned 'em down. I quit baseball for something better."

Another kiss welded her to the spot.

&

Mason hadn't intended to do that. The kiss, the clutch—neither of them was supposed to happen. This was his party, and he was in charge.

Jumping to his feet, he reached for the bottle of mineral water. After several botched attempts, he opened it despite his shaking hands. Somehow he poured water into the glasses, steeling himself with a deep breath before turning to face Blair. And there she sat, slightly disheveled and so beautiful.

"You planned all of this, didn't you?" she said.

"I'm afraid so. But I can explain."

"You're not dumping me for anyone else?"

"Hardly," he said with a chuckle.

He handed her the glass and sank into the chair beside her, knowing if he came any closer he'd never remember the speech he'd rehearsed over and over in his mind. Studying the rising lime in his glass, he took a deep breath and plunged in.

"Okay, here's the deal. The only thing I want is for you and me and Sam to be a family. I bought this place, and Trey set up the deal with Davenport, a buddy of his from prep school. Hannah Andrews gave up a good job as my housekeeper to sit out here in the middle of nowhere and keep an eye on you while I survived on toast and turkey sandwiches. See—I did it all for you. For us. So we could raise horses and kids."

He chanced a look in her direction, nearly losing his nerve as he saw a tear shimmer in her bluebonnet eyes. "Blair, don't cry. Anything but that."

"Honey Hill is yours? Mrs. Andrews is your housekeeper, and Trey is pals with Griffin Davenport?" Her eyes widened, and he waited for the big explosion. "You set this up?"

He felt like such a jerk for bringing her here under false pretenses. He'd blown it but good—that was for sure.

Too late to turn back now. "Yeah, I did."

He knelt beside her, ignoring the sharp slice of pain that shot upward from his worn-out knee. "I love you, Blair. I can't think of a time in my life when I didn't."

"I love you too," she whispered.

This time he was the one to silence her with a kiss. And it felt good, he thought, to be back in control.

Okay, so the Lord was in control, but he was definitely on His side. Mason could have kissed Blair longer, but he stopped, reminding himself of the real reason he'd planned this little party. The other party, the one that started in less than an hour, would celebrate the successful completion of his mission with two hundred of their closest friends.

At least he hoped so.

"Blair?"

She looked up, her eyes still moist. "Hmm?"

"About us." Where were the smooth words he'd planned? "I need to ask you something."

She smiled a lazy smile that sent his heart into overdrive. "What?" came out sounding like a whisper.

Mason put a finger beneath her chin and lifted her face until he gazed into her eyes. For what seemed like an eternity, he stared, unable to call forth the speech he'd practiced. Finally, the words came, and he said them quickly before they could vanish again.

"Will you marry me—again?"

Mason handed her the gift and watched in anticipation while she opened it. She lifted the lid of the small wooden box, the one Sam had taken great delight in painting with blue flowers for the occasion, and gasped.

Wrapped in the folds of the worn green fabric was an engagement ring, a large round diamond mounted on a gold band.

"Yes," she said. "I'll marry you—again."

Then the sprinklers came on.

LUIGI'S ITALIAN MEAT SAUCE A LA BONNIE SUE

2 tablespoons olive oil or salad oil
1 pound ground beef
2 cloves garlic, minced
½ cup of onion slices
2 16-ounce cans (4 cups) tomatoes (I cut these up)
2 8-ounce cans (2 cups) seasoned tomato sauce
1 3-ounce can (⅔ cup) broiled sliced mushrooms
¼ cup chopped parsley
1½ teaspoons oregano or sage (I like oregano)
1 teaspoon salt
¼ teaspoon thyme
1 bay leaf
1 cup water

In a large skillet, cook onion in hot oil till almost tender. Add meat and garlic; brown lightly. Add remaining ingredients. Simmer uncovered 2 to 2½ hours or till sauce is nice and thick; stir occasionally. Remove bay leaf. Serve over hot spaghetti. Pass bowl of shredded Parmesan cheese. Makes 6 servings. Note: One pound of spaghetti noodles will serve 4 to 6 as a main dish with sauce.

A Letter To Our Readers

Dear Reader:

In order that we might better contribute to your reading enjoyment, we would appreciate your taking a few minutes to respond to the following questions. We welcome your comments and read each form and letter we receive. When completed, please return to the following:

Fiction Editor
Heartsong Presents
PO Box 719
Uhrichsville, Ohio 44683

1. Did you enjoy reading *Major League Dad* by Kathleen Y'Barbo?
   ❑ Very much! I would like to see more books by this author!
   ❑ Moderately. I would have enjoyed it more if

   _____

   _____

   _____

2. Are you a member of **Heartsong Presents**? ❑ Yes ❑ No
   If no, where did you purchase this book? _____

   _____

3. How would you rate, on a scale from 1 (poor) to 5 (superior), the cover design? _____

4. On a scale from 1 (poor) to 10 (superior), please rate the following elements.

   ____ Heroine   ____ Plot
   ____ Hero   ____ Inspirational theme
   ____ Setting   ____ Secondary characters

5. These characters were special because?_____

_____

_____

6. How has this book inspired your life?_____

_____

_____

7. What settings would you like to see covered in future
   Heartsong Presents books? _____

_____

_____

8. What are some inspirational themes you would like to see
   treated in future books? _____

_____

_____

9. Would you be interested in reading other **Heartsong
   Presents** titles? ❑ Yes ❑ No

10. Please check your age range:
    ❑ Under 18   ❑ 18-24
    ❑ 25-34   ❑ 35-45
    ❑ 46-55   ❑ Over 55

Name_____

Occupation _____

Address _____

City_____ State_____ Zip_____

$\mathcal{H}$EARTSONG ♥ PRESENTS

Love Stories Are Rated G!

That's for godly, gratifying, and of course, great! If you love a thrilling love story but don't appreciate the sordidness of some popular paperback romances, **Heartsong Presents** is for you. In fact, **Heartsong Presents** is the only inspirational romance book club featuring love stories where Christian faith is the primary ingredient in a marriage relationship.

Sign up today to receive your first set of four, never-before-published Christian romances. Send no money now; you will receive a bill with the first shipment. You may cancel at any time without obligation, and if you aren't completely satisfied with any selection, you may return the books for an immediate refund!

Imagine. . .four new romances every four weeks—two historical, two contemporary—with men and women like you who long to meet the one God has chosen as the love of their lives. . .all for the low price of $10.99 postpaid.

To join, simply complete the coupon below and mail to the address provided. **Heartsong Presents** romances are rated G for another reason: They'll arrive Godspeed!

YES! Sign me up for Heart♥ng!

NEW MEMBERSHIPS WILL BE SHIPPED IMMEDIATELY!
Send no money now. We'll bill you only $10.99 postpaid with your first shipment of four books. Or for faster action, call toll free 1-800-847-8270.

NAME _____

ADDRESS _____

CITY _____ STATE _____ ZIP _____

MAIL TO: HEARTSONG PRESENTS, P.O. Box 721, Uhrichsville, Ohio 44683
or visit www.heartsongpresents.com